An angry sea . . .

Elizabeth pulled her sweater over her head and plunged into the water, steeling herself against the waves that pounded her body. Finally she took a deep breath and dove in, swimming through the icy water in her shorts and T-shirt.

She stroked hard against the waves that kept pushing her back toward the shore. Salt water stung her eyes, but she kept them open anyway, determined not to lose sight of Denny's body.

The water was getting deeper now, and the waves were breaking all around her.

Crash!

White foam spilled over her head, and the force of the huge wave that collapsed on top of her was enough to push her under. She held her breath and fought the undertow, struggling back to the surface.

As soon as her head broke the surface, she opened her eyes and looked frantically for Denny. But there was no sign of him. Where was he?

Bantam Skylark Books in the SWEET VALLEY TWINS AND FRIENDS series.
Ask your bookseller for the books you have missed.

SWEET VALLEY TWINS
AND FRIENDS

Elizabeth the Hero

◇

Written by
Jamie Suzanne

Created by
FRANCINE PASCAL

A BANTAM SKYLARK BOOK ®
NEW YORK • TORONTO • LONDON • SYDNEY • AUCKLAND

RL 4, 008-012

ELIZABETH THE HERO
A Bantam Skylark Book / November 1993

Sweet Valley High® and Sweet Valley Twins and Friends® are
registered trademarks of Francine Pascal

Conceived by Francine Pascal

Produced by Daniel Weiss Associates, Inc.
33 West 17th Street
New York, NY 10011

Cover art by James Mathewuse

Skylark Books is a registered trademark of Bantam Books, a division of
Bantam Doubleday Dell Publishing Group, Inc.
Registered in U.S. Patent and Trademark Office and elsewhere.

ISBN: 0-553-48060-X

Published simultaneously in the United States and Canada

Bantam Books are published by Bantam Books, a division of Bantam
Doubleday Dell Publishing Group, Inc. Its trademark, consisting of the
words "Bantam Books" and the portrayal of a rooster, is Registered in
U.S. Patent and Trademark Office and in other countries. Marca
Registrada. Bantam Books, 1540 Broadway, New York, New York 10036.

PRINTED IN THE UNITED STATES OF AMERICA

OPM   0 9 8 7 6 5 4 3 2 1

Elizabeth
the Hero

One

"Look at this one!" Amy Sutton cried excitedly. She bent over and scooped a light-pink shell up out of the sand.

"That's gorgeous," Maria Slater said.

"It's not even chipped," Elizabeth Wakefield pointed out.

Maria held the bucket out toward Amy, who carefully put the pink shell on top of the others they had collected.

Elizabeth dug her toes down into the sand. She loved being at the beach late on a Friday afternoon. Especially on a day like today, when the wind was up and the surf was booming. It was practically deserted.

"This seashell collage is going to be great," Maria commented. "I never realized shells came in so many different shapes and colors. Mr. Sweeny is going to love it." She scratched her nose and left a little trail of sand along the smooth brown skin of her pretty face.

Maria and Amy were two of Elizabeth's best friends. All three of them were in the sixth grade at Sweet Valley Middle School, and also in the same art class.

"Elizabeth's ideas for art projects are always good," Amy said, pushing her straight, dark-blond hair out of her eyes.

Elizabeth smiled. "You know me. Perfect in every way." She laughed. "I just hope we can arrange these shells into some kind of design that will look as nice on paper as they do on the beach."

A sudden gust of wind lifted Elizabeth's long blond hair and swirled it around her face. She brushed it back, glancing up at the sky. "Uh-oh. Look at those dark clouds over there." She shivered. "It looks like there's a storm moving in."

"It feels like it to me. Look," Amy said, pointing out toward the water. "The waves are even higher than when we got here."

Maria put her hand over her eyes and squinted. "Look at those people out there surfing!"

Elizabeth searched the rough, dark water and spotted two small figures wearing neon-colored wet suits, paddling out into the foam on surfboards.

"I'm pretty sure that's Denny Jacobson and his brother, Sam," Amy said. "I recognize Denny's red wet suit."

Denny Jacobson was an eighth-grader at Sweet Valley Middle School. His brother, Sam, was a sophomore at Sweet Valley High. As the girls watched, a large wave broke over the boys' surfboards. "Oh no!" Elizabeth cried as the two figures disappeared from sight. Then she let out a sigh of relief when she saw the boys reappear, apparently unhurt, and still paddling out.

"Why are they surfing in weather like this?" Maria asked. "The water looks really rough."

"Because they're cowboy surfers," Amy said. "They love going out in terrible weather."

"I wish they'd come back in," Elizabeth said nervously. She knew the weather was getting more dangerous, yet the boys kept paddling out into deeper and deeper water. "In my lifesaving course, the first thing they taught us was that the best way to save a life was not to risk your own."

Just then a strong current began to carry Denny away from Sam. "I wish they'd come back in too," Maria said with a shiver. "Just watching them scares me."

Amy shook her head. "So let's not watch. Come on. Let's walk back the other way and catch the bus home."

Amy and Maria started walking away, but Elizabeth stayed right where she was. She could see the current carrying Denny even farther away from his brother, but Sam didn't seem to notice. He kept paddling straight out to sea.

"They need to stay closer together," Elizabeth muttered. Amy and Maria stopped and watched with

Elizabeth as Denny turned his board back toward the shore, preparing to catch a wave. Elizabeth felt her heart pounding as Denny began to paddle faster and faster, the huge wave rising up behind him.

White foam appeared along the ridge of the wave as it formed a curl. Denny hopped up on his board and squatted. Then, slowly and carefully, he stood.

"He's amazing," Amy whispered.

Denny really did look good. His body was balanced gracefully and expertly on the board as he rode the wave.

But he began to teeter as the wave curled higher and higher behind him.

"Watch out!" Elizabeth yelled, even though she knew he couldn't hear her.

Denny didn't look back, and didn't realize the wave was breaking until the tall, foaming wall crashed down over him and brutally knocked him off of his board.

"Noooo!" Amy gasped.

Maria's hands flew to her mouth.

Denny struggled to swim in the churning water while the surfboard flew into the air and flipped over like a dolphin. The board seem to hover in the air for a moment, its wet surface catching the light like a mirror. And then it rapidly spiraled downward.

"No!" Amy shrieked again.

As they watched in horror, the surfboard plunged downward and hit Denny hard on the head. Denny's body disappeared beneath the surface as a second wave came crashing down and sent the board skipping and hopping across the water.

All three girls raced to the edge of the water, their eyes frantically searching the sea, waiting for Denny to come up for air.

"Where is he?" Maria cried after a few tense moments.

Elizabeth put her hand to her eyes to block the sun, squinting out over the waves. "There he is!" she said suddenly. "See?"

"He's not swimming," Amy whispered.

Denny appeared to be motionless. He looked like a limp, empty wet suit bobbing on the surface.

"He's unconscious!" Maria cried.

"*Sam!*" Elizabeth screamed. "*Sam!*" She frantically waved her arms, trying to attract Sam's attention.

But Sam was several hundred feet away from Denny, lying on his stomach on his own surfboard, paddling out in the opposite direction.

"SAM!" all three girls screamed at the tops of their lungs.

But the wind carried their voices up and away.

"Here comes another one," Amy croaked.

Another wave loomed up over Denny. There was a crashing sound accompanied by a burst of white foam as the wave broke and tossed Denny's limp body around like a rag doll.

Elizabeth kicked off her shoes and began to run.

"Elizabeth! What are you doing?" she heard Amy scream as she ran for the water. She didn't answer or turn around. She didn't have time. Every second counted now.

Elizabeth pulled her sweater over her head and plunged into the water, steeling herself against the waves that pounded her body. Finally she took a deep breath and dove in, swimming through the icy water in her shorts and T-shirt.

She stroked hard against the waves that kept pushing her back toward the shore. Salt water stung her eyes, but she kept them open anyway, determined not to lose sight of Denny's body.

The water was getting deeper now, and the waves were breaking all around her.

Crash!

White foam spilled over her head, and the force of the huge wave collapsing on top of her pushed her underwater. She held her breath and fought the undertow, struggling back to the surface.

As soon as her head broke the surface, she opened her eyes and looked frantically for Denny. But there was no sign of him. Where was he?

Finally she spotted him. He was floating several yards away—facedown!

Without hesitating, Elizabeth swam toward Denny, slicing through the water as fear gave her limbs new strength. When she reached him, she bent her arm around his head and turned his face so that it pointed upward, out of the water. That was what she'd learned to do in her lifesaving course. Then she cupped his chin with her hand and began to tow him back to shore.

Kick! Kick! Kick! Elizabeth ordered herself. Her legs felt like lead, and she was almost sobbing with fatigue. She had never been so exhausted in her life. Still, she knifed her legs in and out of the water, trying desperately to propel herself and Denny toward shore.

Denny's eyes were closed, and Elizabeth wondered if, subconsciously, he had any idea how desperately she was struggling for their lives. There was a hard current pulling her out to sea, but Elizabeth was determined to beat it. And determined not to let go of Denny.

Kick! Kick! Kick! She had to keep going. Keep kicking. There was no choice. Their only hope of surviving lay in her ability to keep kicking.

It's only a few more yards, she told herself. *Just a few more yards.*

But it wasn't. It was a long, long way to shore.

She could see Maria and Amy standing ankle-deep in the water, waving and shouting encouragement.

"Don't give up!" she heard Amy shout. "You can do it! I know you can do it!"

Amy's voice sounded high and thin in the wind, but her words gave Elizabeth new courage and determination.

Suddenly her legs didn't feel quite so heavy. Amy was right. She *could* do it. And she would.

Kick! Kick! Kick!

Finally, after what seemed like hours, she reached

the shallow water, and Amy and Maria came dashing out to help her. Together, the three girls dragged Denny's body out of the surf and up onto the sand.

"Denny! What happened?" Sam was running toward them now. He'd seen them and paddled in.

Elizabeth collapsed on the sand, choking and exhausted as Sam knelt down next to Denny.

"What do you want us to do?" Amy asked in a tense voice.

"Go call for help," Elizabeth gasped, gulping air into her aching lungs.

She heard the pounding of Amy's feet on the sand as she raced toward the road that ran behind the beach. Sam held Denny's hand, and Maria hovered anxiously.

"What are you going to do?" Sam asked Elizabeth as she positioned Denny's head and placed her hands on his chest.

"I'm going to give him mouth-to-mouth resuscitation," she answered. She tried to sound confident, but her heart was pounding with terror. She'd paid close attention in the lifesaving class. But would she remember everything correctly?

Elizabeth took several deep breaths to calm herself. Then she bent down, pressed her mouth to Denny's, and began the sequence of breathing and pushing motions that she had been taught.

After a few agonizingly tense moments, Denny gave a great big cough.

"*All right!*" Sam yelled.

Elizabeth sat back on her heels, and Denny coughed again, bringing up some of the water that had lodged in his lungs.

"He's OK!" Maria called out. "He's going to be OK!"

"You did it," Sam breathed, his terrified face beginning to relax. "You saved him!"

Elizabeth nodded, and then fell back on the sand in an exhausted heap.

Two

"I am, too, popular with the boys," Ellen Riteman insisted.

Janet Howell made a superior face. "I didn't say you weren't, Ellen. I just said you're not as popular as I am. Just take Denny Jacobson, for example. He's probably the most popular guy in the middle school, and he obviously likes me more than anyone else."

The members of the Unicorn Club had been arguing for fifteen minutes about which one of them was the most popular with boys. Janet was in the eighth grade and the president of the club. Being self-confident was part of being a Unicorn, but Janet sometimes took it a little too far.

"Let's just agree that all the Unicorns are popular with boys and move on. We're not getting anything accomplished here," Mandy Miller said impatiently.

Jessica Wakefield looked around at the group of girls gathered in her living room. Next to her on the sofa were Mandy and Mary Wallace. Grace Oliver, Tamara Chase, and Kimberly Haver sat on the floor. Janet sat in the big, comfortable wing chair, and Lila Fowler sat on the footstool of the wing chair.

It was late in the afternoon and Jessica had invited the Unicorn Club over for their weekly meeting. The Unicorns were the prettiest and most popular girls at Sweet Valley Middle School. They loved boys and parties and clothes and gossip, and most of all, they loved being the center of attention—especially when the attention came from boys.

Jessica loved being a member of the Unicorn Club, and sometimes she wished Elizabeth, her identical twin sister, were a member too. Elizabeth had been asked to join the club a long time ago, but she had dropped out after one meeting. She thought the Unicorns were silly and superficial, and secretly called them the "snob squad." She liked reading and hanging out with her friends much more than chasing—or being chased by—boys. But in spite of their differences, Elizabeth was Jessica's very best friend.

"I agree with Mandy," Mary said. "Let's get on with the meeting."

"Tell us about the Teen Health Fair," Tamara said.

"Right," Grace echoed. "Have you decided who you're going to pick to be hostesses?"

The Teen Health Fair was held every year at the downtown auditorium. This year, as in previous years, there would be a number of booths and exhibits, all relating to teen-health topics. One student from each school in the county was invited to give a short speech. Janet had been chosen to represent Sweet Valley Middle School, and the topic of her speech was *You and Orthodontia*. Since Janet had recently gotten a night gear to straighten her teeth, she knew a lot about the subject.

As the Teen Health Fair Representative, Janet was also in charge of picking a few girls to be hostesses. The hostesses got to wear special armbands, man the booths, and circulate throughout the auditorium, giving people directions and handing out leaflets. There would be tons of kids there from other schools in the county—and that meant tons of boys. Janet had heard there might even be local television coverage. That's why Jessica and the other Unicorns wanted to be chosen so badly.

In typical Janet Howell fashion, she had turned the whole thing into a competition, forcing the Unicorn Club members to run her errands and do her work. Jessica had spent hours in the library researching the history of orthodontia for Janet's speech.

But even after all that work, Jessica was worried she wouldn't be chosen. Mandy and Mary had really gone all out. They had constructed a giant papier-mâché molar in Janet's garage. It was hollow, so that somebody could get inside it and walk around the auditorium. Janet said she thought the tooth costume would raise people's consciousness. But Jessica had a feeling Janet wouldn't be caught dead walking around in the thing herself.

Please choose me as a hostess, Jessica pleaded silently. *And please don't ask me to be the tooth.*

Janet cleared her throat and sat up straighter. "I don't want to make any snap decisions," she announced. "It's important that I choose the right girls to represent Sweet Valley Middle School."

Everybody groaned. This was typical Janet too, Jessica reflected bitterly. She obviously wanted to wait until the last possible minute to decide.

"The Teen Health Fair is one of the major events of the year. I know everyone at school is looking forward to it. And a lot of guys have gone out of their way to tell me how much they're looking forward to hearing my speech." She smiled smugly. "Especially Denny Jacobson."

Jessica felt Mary's elbow nudge her in the ribs. When she looked at Mary, Mary rolled her eyes and Jessica couldn't help smiling.

Janet had a huge crush on Denny Jacobson, and she talked about him all the time.

"Denny made a point of telling me that his father had worn braces when he was a teenager." She tossed her hair over her shoulder. "You know Denny, he's always finding some excuse to talk to me."

Ding dong!

The sound of the doorbell made Jessica jump. She realized she'd nearly drifted off. Saved by the bell—

falling asleep in a Unicorn Club meeting certainly *wouldn't* have impressed Janet. Jessica heard her mother's footsteps on the stairs. She heard the door open, and several voices talking at once.

"*Elizabeth!*" she heard her mother exclaim. "Sarah! Bill! . . . Ned! . . ." she heard her shout to Mr. Wakefield, who was working in the study off the front hall. "Ned! Please come quickly. The Jacobsons are here. And they've brought Elizabeth."

The alarm in her mother's voice made Jessica jump up and run to the front hall to see what was going on. Several of her friends scrambled up and followed her.

When Jessica saw the group standing just inside the front door she gasped. "Lizzie!" she shrieked. "What happened?"

Elizabeth was standing in the doorway, soaking wet and wrapped in a blanket. With her were Denny's parents, Sarah and Bill Jacobson. Mrs. Jacobson had her arm around Elizabeth, and all three of them looked pale and shaken.

"Your daughter saved Denny's life this afternoon," Mrs. Jacobson said to Mr. and Mrs. Wakefield in a voice choked with emotion.

Behind her, Jessica heard Janet gasp.

"He and Sam were out surfing in a very rough sea, and Denny fell and hit his head on his board," Mr. Jacobson continued.

"Oh no," Janet moaned.

"Elizabeth risked her life to swim out in that dangerous water and bring Denny back to shore," Mrs. Jacobson continued. "Thank God she knows how to give mouth-to-mouth resuscitation."

There was a long, stunned silence as everybody stared at Elizabeth. Suddenly Mrs. Wakefield threw her arms around Elizabeth, and everybody started talking at once.

Jessica was trying to listen to the Jacobsons, to Elizabeth, and to her parents, but it was hard with everybody talking at the same time. Something about waves, and undertows, and almost drowning.

It sounded like something out of a movie. Elizabeth, her very own identical twin sister, had saved Denny Jacobson from drowning. Elizabeth was a hero!

Denny was fine now, according to his parents, but the doctors wanted to keep him at the hospital overnight just to be sure. The Jacobsons had just come from the hospital to bring Elizabeth home. They were returning immediately to be with Denny.

"We'll come with you," Mrs. Wakefield said, reaching out and taking Mrs. Jacobson's hand. "Won't we, Ned?"

"You bet," Mr. Wakefield answered. "I know you're pretty shaken up after what happened. You could probably use some company."

"Can Denny have company?" Janet asked quickly.

Mrs. Jacobson hesitated. "Well . . . yes . . . I suppose so." She smiled at Elizabeth, tears gathering in her eyes. It looked as if she were about to cry. "I know he would like Elizabeth to come back with us—if she feels up to it."

"Sure," Elizabeth said with a wan smile.

Mrs. Wakefield put her arm around Elizabeth's shoulders. "Come upstairs and change clothes. Then we'll all go to the hospital. And we'll drive some of the girls if they want to go."

"You're a hero, Elizabeth," Mandy said softly, echoing Jessica's thoughts. "A real hero."

"No, I'm not," Elizabeth managed. She was holding the blanket tightly around her shoulders and her teeth were chattering. Jessica noticed that Elizabeth's face looked pale under the damp strands of hair that hung around her face. She reached over and squeezed Elizabeth's hand, feeling incredibly proud of her sister.

"You're a hero to us," Mrs. Jacobson said solemnly. "If it hadn't been for you and your quick thinking, Denny might not be alive now."

Three

"You're really lucky, kiddo," Sam said, affectionately ruffling Denny's hair.

Denny grinned and looked around the room. His eyes came to rest on Elizabeth, who gave him a warm smile. Part of her wished she were home in bed, but she knew it must be important to Denny to have his friends with him.

"I am lucky. Lucky to be alive. And lucky to have so many friends. You guys were all really nice to come by."

Denny's hospital room was getting so crowded with friends and well-wishers that some kids had to stand out in the hall. It was hard to breathe in the room, and Elizabeth thought about heading out to the hall herself. But just then Denny motioned for her to come closer.

"Come sit over here, Elizabeth," he said, pointing to a chair near his bed that Janet and Lila were sharing.

"Oh, that's OK, Denny, I'm fine right here."

"No, really. Having you around makes me feel safe, for some reason."

Everyone in the room laughed. Elizabeth made her way through the crowd toward Denny. Janet wasn't showing any sign of budging from the chair, so she sat on the edge of his bed.

Maria gave Elizabeth's arm a little squeeze. Maria and Amy had ridden to the hospital with Sam and Denny, and then stayed while the Jacobsons took Elizabeth home to change.

Elizabeth, Jessica, Janet, Mandy, and Mary had all ridden to the hospital with Mr. and Mrs. Wakefield in their van. It had been a very crowded ride, since Steven, the twins' fourteen-year-old brother, and his girlfriend, Cathy Connors, had come back from the movies just as the van was leaving. As soon as they heard what had happened, they had wanted to come to the hospital too.

Sam had called Rick Hunter, Denny's best friend, to tell him what happened. Rick had called Peter DeHaven, who had called a bunch of other people, and all of them had hurried over to the hospital to make sure Denny was OK.

The room had gotten so crowded that Mr. and Mrs. Wakefield had stayed only long enough to give Denny a hug and say hello. Then they had gone with

Mr. and Mrs. Jacobson to get some coffee in the cafeteria and give the kids a chance to talk.

Denny was fine except for a bump on his head. When Sam ruffled Denny's hair again, Denny grimaced. "Ouch!"

"Sorry," Sam said quickly, his face clouding over with concern.

Immediately Denny broke into a grin. "Don't worry," he joked. "My head's a lot harder than you think. I'm surprised it didn't break the surfboard."

Everybody in the room burst into laughter again, and Denny laughed the loudest of all. His laughter didn't seem completely natural to Elizabeth, though. It was just a little too loud. His eyes were too bright. And his face was so animated it just didn't seem real. He was working too hard at acting as though it was no big deal. It made her realize that he was pretty shaken up.

"What's going on in here?" Denny's doctor appeared at the door with a smile on his face. He made his way through the crowded room toward Denny's bed. "It looks like a party in here."

"If you had just escaped death, you'd want to party too," Denny told the doctor with a grin.

Janet put her hand on Denny's arm. "Denny, I'm so glad you're OK," she said dramatically. "Every time I think about what could have happened to you, I—"

"This is the girl who saved me," Denny said, interrupting Janet. He reached over to take Elizabeth's hand, brushing Janet's arm off the bed.

The doctor stuck a thermometer in Denny's mouth and turned to Elizabeth. "You must be quite a girl," he said. "I know Denny's friends and family are very grateful to you."

"You can't imagine how grateful we are," Janet said quickly before Elizabeth could respond. "I don't know what I would do if Denny were—"

"Lucky thing Elizabeth took that lifesaving course," Sam put in before Janet could finish. "She's a good example for the rest of us. Anybody who hasn't taken the course should sign up."

"I've already called the Pool Club," Janet began, "and they said anybody interested in signing up for the next lifesaving course should go to the Pool Club After School Party. You can pick up registration cards at the snack bar and—"

"Is there an Elizabeth Wakefield here?" A businesslike female voice cut Janet off.

"Here," Elizabeth said, standing up. She looked curiously at the attractive woman who had appeared at the door. As the woman came into the crowded room, Elizabeth noticed that she had a notebook and a large camera.

"How do you do?" the woman said with a smile. "Hospital admissions called me. I'm Juanita Morse, a reporter from the *Sweet Valley Tribune*. I hear you rescued a friend after a surfing accident this afternoon."

"She saved my life," Denny said when the doctor pulled the thermometer from his mouth. "She risked her own life to save mine. I never would have believed that a sixth-grader could swim in waves ten feet high."

"Wow!" Ms. Morse exclaimed. She opened her notebook and began to scribble.

"More like four or five feet," Elizabeth corrected. She was proud of what she had done, but she knew the waves hadn't been ten feet high—even though to Denny, who had been in danger, they had probably seemed enormous.

". . . swam out through waves ten feet high," Ms. Morse muttered as she scribbled in her notebook.

"She *said*, four or five," Janet snapped.

Ms. Morse looked up curiously. "Who are you?" she asked.

Janet broke into a broad grin. "Janet Howell. That's Howell with two l's," she said. "Denny and I have been—"

"Were you on the beach when all this was happening?" Ms. Morse asked.

Janet smirked. "No. I was at a meeting of the Unicorns. The Unicorn Club is—"

But Ms. Morse had lost interest when she realized Janet wasn't an eyewitness to the rescue. "What were you thinking about when you plunged out into those ten-foot waves?" she asked Elizabeth before Janet could finish explaining about the Unicorns.

"More like four to five feet," Elizabeth corrected her. "And actually, I don't know what I was thinking. I can't really remember. All I remember thinking was that Denny was in trouble out there, and that if I didn't go out and bring him back, he was going to drown."

"Ohhh," Janet moaned softly.

Ms. Morse shot a strange look at Janet, then turned her attention back to Denny and smiled. "How about giving me a quote for my story?"

Denny looked at Elizabeth with shining eyes. "You can quote me as saying that Elizabeth Wakefield is my hero."

Ms. Morse lifted her camera. "I'd love to get a picture of this," she said. "Hold those smiles." Her fingers fumbled with the lens. "Hold it . . . hold it . . . Now say—"

"Elizabeth, you've got a piece of hair sticking up," Janet said, reaching toward Elizabeth just as the flashbulb went off.

Ms. Morse gave Janet an annoyed glance. "I think I got a hand in that one. Let's try this one more time."

Janet scowled as Denny put his arm around Elizabeth's shoulders and gave a big smile for the camera.

"That's it. Great," Ms. Morse told them. "Now say . . . hero!"

"Look at this!" Steven shouted. He stood in the doorway of the kitchen, holding up the newspaper.

It was Saturday morning, and Elizabeth, Jessica, and Mr. and Mrs. Wakefield were all seated at the kitchen table, finishing a late breakfast.

"Unbelievable. There's a whole big article on Elizabeth and Denny in here," Steven said.

"Really?" Jessica shrieked. "Let me see." She jumped up from the table and tried to snatch the paper from Steven.

"After me," he said, holding the paper high in the air and out of Jessica's reach.

"Excuse me," Mr. Wakefield said. "But I believe the heads of the household customarily get first crack at the morning paper. So how about handing it over?"

"Wait a minute," Steven said. "Let me just look at the picture."

Elizabeth tapped her water glass with her spoon. "Not that it has anything to do with me or anything, but would anybody mind if *I* took a look?"

Mr. and Mrs. Wakefield started laughing. Mr. Wakefield got up, took the paper from Steven, and spread it out on the counter. "Come on," he said. "Let's all read it together."

Everyone hung over Mr. Wakefield's shoulder and gazed proudly at the large photo of Elizabeth and Denny.

"'Local girl braves ten-foot waves to save friend,'" Steven read from the caption.

Elizabeth groaned inwardly. She couldn't understand what the problem was. The story had been written by this supposedly professional journalist. "Why couldn't they get the facts straight? The waves were four or maybe five feet high. Saying the waves were ten feet high makes me sound like I'm some kind of Supergirl."

Mrs. Wakefield laughed. "You're definitely a super-girl to us, sweetie."

"Our lives will never be the same," Steven said. "First come the reporters, then—"

"A miniseries on TV," Jessica finished for him. "I get to play Elizabeth."

Mrs. Wakefield reached into one of the kitchen drawers and removed a pair of scissors. "I'll cut this out for the family scrapbook," she said.

"Our house will be on the tour of Stars' Homes," Jessica went on. "They'll make a little detour from Beverly Hills."

"Jessica," Elizabeth said, unable to hide her smile. "Would you cut it out?"

"I'm sorry, Lizzie. But I'm serious. You did a really great thing. And you're not even appreciating all the attention you're getting."

Elizabeth shrugged. The truth was, she did feel a little proud. Denny was alive, and she had had something to do with that. "Sure I am. I'm just mad because I want to play *myself* in the miniseries."

Late that afternoon, Elizabeth sat on her bed, propped up against her yellow and blue throw pillows with her math homework in her lap.

She looked up at the lifesaving certificate that was tacked to her bulletin board, and smiled. Every student who had completed the lifesaving course at the Sweet Valley Pool Club had received one.

She'd never dreamed at the time that she would be

using those lifesaving techniques so soon. She closed her eyes and shivered, remembering the hard tug of the current and the way the waves had pounded her. Actually saving someone from the ocean was a lot different than practicing in the pool—where there was a lifeguard handy in case you got in trouble.

Elizabeth hadn't told anyone this, but there had been a moment or two when she had been afraid she might not make it back to shore herself.

There had been so much going on last night and this morning, she hadn't had time to think very much about it. But now that she was sitting here remembering it, reliving it . . . what had happened gave her a shaky, scared feeling in the pit of her stomach.

Elizabeth opened her eyes and tried to concentrate on the warm beam of sunlight that streamed in the window. She sank back deeper into her pillows, pushing the memory of the cold water and the pounding waves to the back of her mind. The sooner people stopped talking about it, the better, she decided.

Elizabeth wasn't used to being the center of attention, and hearing herself described as a hero made her feel like a phony. Now that she realized how scared she had actually been, she didn't feel very heroic at all.

A soft knock interrupted her thoughts.

"Come in," Elizabeth called.

The door opened and a familiar face peeped in. "May I come in?" Cathy Connors asked.

"Sure," Elizabeth said. She and Jessica both liked Cathy a lot. They had played a big part in getting Steven and Cathy together.

"Steven and I are going to the beach," Cathy said, coming over and sitting down on the edge of Elizabeth's bed. "But I just wanted to tell you again how terrific I think you are. I read the story about you and Denny in the paper this morning. The picture was really cute. I wish they had run it in the Sunday paper so more people could have seen it."

"I'm kind of glad it was in the paper today," Elizabeth said quickly. "There are almost two whole days between now and Monday. Maybe that will give people enough time to stop talking about it so much."

Cathy laughed. "I know one person who'll never forget about it—Denny Jacobson."

"Oh, sure he will. He has a whole life of surfing ahead of him," Elizabeth said. "He's not going to think about the accident for very long."

Cathy smiled. "We'll see."

"That's right," Jessica said breathlessly. "Fifteen-foot waves . . . uh-huh . . . uh-huh . . . Rain and lightning? Welllll . . . it may not have been lightning—*exactly*—but the water was *very* choppy."

Elizabeth came upstairs just in time to overhear Jessica talking on the hall telephone. "Jessica!" she said ominously.

"I'll call you back later," Jessica said, quickly hanging up the phone.

"Who was that?" Elizabeth demanded.

"Aaron Dallas," Jessica said, breaking into a broad smile. "He's totally impressed with your amazing rescue."

"It wasn't amazing," Elizabeth protested. "The waves *were not* that high. And there wasn't any rain or lightning. I thought I was the creative writer in this family."

"Well, there might have been," Jessica said. "And even if there had been," she added proudly, "I'll bet it wouldn't have stopped you. You would have swum right out into that tidal wave and—"

"*Tidal wave!* Jessica!" She stamped her foot impatiently. "Why are you exaggerating everything?"

"It makes a better story that way," Jessica said with a grin.

"You mean a lie," Elizabeth shot back.

Jessica crossed her arms over her chest. "If I'm going to be related to a hero, I want to be related to a *big* hero."

"What Elizabeth did was quite heroic enough," Mr. Wakefield said as he came out of his bedroom. "If you don't think so, ask the Jacobsons. I think they're pretty happy that their son is alive and well."

"*Pretty happy?*" Jessica said with a giggle. "They thanked Elizabeth about a thousand times. They probably would have given Elizabeth their car if she'd asked for it."

Mr. Wakefield raised an eyebrow. "Come on, Jess, wouldn't you thank somebody a thousand times if they saved Elizabeth's life?"

"Of course, Dad," Jessica replied, rolling her eyes.

"What if they saved me?" Steven asked, coming out of his room.

"I'd tell them to throw you back," Jessica retorted.

"Ha ha," Steven said sarcastically.

"Hey," Mr. Wakefield said sharply. "Under the circumstances, I'm not sure that's funny. Apologize to your brother."

"I'm sorry," Jessica muttered.

"I don't think you realize just how serious a tragedy this might have been," Mr. Wakefield said. "If your sister hadn't gone out into that water . . ."

Elizabeth sighed and listened miserably as her father recounted, once again, the story of the dramatic rescue.

Why couldn't he forget about it? Why couldn't they all at least stop talking about it?

Four

"Who wants pancakes?" Mr. Wakefield asked as he poured large circles of batter into the skillet. "And how many?"

"Six for me," Steven shouted, hurtling into the kitchen with his backpack. He dropped it on the counter and then sat down at the breakfast table.

"Jessica? Elizabeth?"

"Six," Jessica said, taking the orange juice out of the refrigerator.

"*Jessica!*"

"OK. Four."

It was Monday morning, and Mr. Wakefield was making breakfast. Mr. Wakefield was an attorney, and Elizabeth always got a big kick out of watching him prepare breakfast in his suit. He put his tie very carefully over his shoulder and covered his white shirt and his slacks with a long chef's apron that she and Jessica and Steven had given him for his birthday.

Mrs. Wakefield was still upstairs, getting ready for work. Their mother was a part-time interior designer, and she had a meeting with a client that morning.

"I'll have four pancakes, please," Elizabeth said with a smile. Sitting at the round table in the kitchen, she had a perfect view out into the backyard through the big glass window. It was a beautiful day, cool and sunny. Elizabeth was looking forward to the walk to school.

"Four pancakes coming right up," Mr. Wakefield said.

"On second thought, I'll take five." Elizabeth loved her father's pancakes. Usually she could only eat four. But this morning she'd awakened with a big appetite.

"We're going to have to call a tow truck to haul you to school," Steven said. "You must have really hit the books last night."

Elizabeth rolled her eyes at Steven, but she didn't answer. It hadn't been homework that kept her awake last night. It had been dreams. Bad dreams. Nightmares in which she was trying desperately to pull Denny to shore. A shore that drifted farther and farther away, the harder she swam. Denny was screaming, screaming something about how she was supposed to save him, it was her job to save him, she couldn't let him down, she couldn't let him drown.

Just thinking about it made her shudder.

Suddenly the doorbell rang.

"I'll get it," Steven shouted, jumping up from his seat and racing out of the kitchen so fast he practically knocked over Mrs. Wakefield as she came into the kitchen.

"It's probably the boy collecting for the newspaper," she called out after Steven. "The money is in the top drawer of the chest in the hall. Give him a tip."

"OK," Steven said from the hall.

Mrs. Wakefield smiled at the girls as she sat down at the table. "Good morning." Her eyes rested on Elizabeth's face and she frowned slightly. "Is everything all right, Elizabeth? You look a little pale to me."

"That's because she was up late studying," Jessica said, pouring her mother a glass of orange juice.

"How many pancakes, honey?" Mr. Wakefield asked.

Before Mrs. Wakefield could answer, Steven appeared back in the kitchen with a funny look on his face. "Elizabeth," he said, sounding as though he was trying not to laugh. "Denny's here to see you."

Elizabeth looked up and saw Denny step into the kitchen. Clutched in his hand was a little spray of flowers.

"These are for you," he explained, holding the bouquet forward.

"Gee, Denny," she said, feeling uncomfortable. "You didn't have to bring me flowers."

"I wanted to," he said solemnly. "It's the least I can do."

Elizabeth heard muffled laughter from Steven's direction and looked over just in time to see him hurry from the room.

There was another sound from Jessica's direction. A snort. Elizabeth saw her twin's hand fly to her face—almost, but not quite in time to cover her twitching lips. Elizabeth felt a flush creeping up her neck. Denny's unexpected visit—with flowers—was embarrassing enough without her family watching.

"I think that's very nice, Denny," Mrs. Wakefield said, darting a stern look at Jessica.

Jessica bit her lip and dropped her eyes to her plate.

Elizabeth reached out, took the flowers, and gave them an appreciative sniff. "Thanks, Denny. But you really didn't need to do this."

"Are you kidding? Not bring flowers to the girl who risked her own life to pull me out of ten-foot waves?"

"Four or five feet," Elizabeth, Jessica, and Mr. and Mrs. Wakefield all said at once.

"Whatever," Denny said with a wave of his hand. "All I know is that I wouldn't be alive today if it weren't for you. I know I'll never be able to repay you for what you did, but I want to do whatever I can. And I'm going to start by carrying your books to school. I'm going to carry them *every day*."

"You don't need to do that," Elizabeth insisted. Denny was nice and everything, but she didn't want him walking her to school every day. He wasn't her boyfriend. And if he started paying a whole lot of attention to her, people would tease her about it.

Besides, she didn't want him reminding her of the rescue all the time. It was strange, but thinking about it made her feel nervous, almost as though *she* were drowning. "To tell you the truth, I don't want you to try to repay me. It was nothing. Really."

"Nothing!" Denny exclaimed.

"Ahem!"

Elizabeth looked up quickly and saw her mother trying to catch her eye. Mrs. Wakefield nodded her head almost imperceptibly in the direction of the dining room. "Elizabeth, dear," she said in a sweet voice. "May I speak to you for just a moment?"

"Sure," Elizabeth said. She smiled at Denny. "I'll be back in a second." She stood up and followed her mother into the dining room.

Mrs. Wakefield closed the door and motioned to Elizabeth to come closer so that they could talk without being overheard in the kitchen. "I know you're just being modest," she began, "but when you tell Denny that saving his life was nothing, it sounds as if you don't think his life is very important."

"Mom!" Elizabeth protested. That wasn't what she had meant at all.

Her mother put her finger to her lips. "Shhh," she warned. "I think you should just let Denny walk you to school if he wants to."

"Every day?" Elizabeth burst out.

Mrs. Wakefield smiled. "Denny's feelings are very

natural. You saved his life, and he's grateful. He wants to do something for you. But don't worry. He'll probably stick close for a day or two, and then he'll get over it." She laughed. "Even the most intense gratitude has a way of wearing off eventually."

"But I feel kind of embarrassed," Elizabeth explained. "To be honest, I don't like being reminded of how I rescued him every second. It reminds me that I'm not very brave at all. I didn't feel brave while it was happening. I felt scared," she confided. "Really scared. That's not very heroic."

Mrs. Wakefield ran her hand over Elizabeth's hair. "Your feelings are very natural too. But you know something? It takes more bravery to do something you're afraid of than it does to do something that doesn't frighten you."

Elizabeth sighed.

"Trust me," Mrs. Wakefield said in a reassuring tone. "It's a phase. He'll get over it. In the meantime, enjoy a little hero worship. You've earned it."

When Elizabeth came back into the kitchen, her father was on his way upstairs to find his briefcase. Denny was sitting at the glass-topped breakfast table, talking and laughing with Steven and Jessica.

As soon as he saw Elizabeth, he stood up and came over to her.

Elizabeth forced herself to smile at Denny. "It's really nice of you to walk me to school," she said. "Thanks for coming over."

"Hey, no problem. Like I said, it's the least I can do." He eyed Elizabeth's backpack on the kitchen floor and picked it up. It was pretty heavy, but Denny hoisted it onto his shoulder along with his own backpack. "Ready to go?"

"Well, ahhhh, not really . . ." Elizabeth began. She hadn't finished her breakfast, and she usually liked to brush her teeth after she ate.

Denny grabbed her arm. "Come on, Elizabeth. Let's get going. I can't wait to tell everybody at school about how amazing you were on Friday."

The next thing she knew, Denny was propelling her through the living room and out the front door.

"But . . . but . . ."

"No buts," he said cheerfully, steering her down the sidewalk.

Elizabeth sighed. She had the feeling a little hero worship was going to go a long way.

". . . and she pulled me back to shore through ten-foot waves," Denny was telling the crossing guard.

The crossing guard stared admiringly at Elizabeth. "Wow! What an incredibly brave thing to do."

"Well," Elizabeth said uneasily, "I wouldn't say that. I just happened to be there, and . . ."

Denny shook his head. "Not only brave—but modest, too."

Honk! Honk!

"Denny," Elizabeth said. "I really think we should go now." Cars were backing up in both directions.

But Denny had insisted on telling the crossing guard the entire story of his rescue—complete with exaggerations.

Honk! Honk!

"Hold your horses!" the guard shouted. "You people are honking at a hero!"

". . . and she was half-dead herself by the time she pulled me back in," Denny finished dramatically.

"My, my," the old man said. "That's an exciting story." He peered at Elizabeth. "You're a very brave girl."

Elizabeth smiled politely, but she felt as if she was going to die of embarrassment. This was the fourth time Denny had told the story this morning. If he didn't stop telling every single person they passed, they were going to be late for school.

She glanced at her watch. "It's getting late," she reminded Denny. "The first bell will be ringing any minute now."

"You're right," Denny said agreeably. He said good-bye to the man, and he and Elizabeth hurried across the street to the school and ran up the front steps.

"Denny!" Janet Howell cried as they came in the front door. "I've been waiting for you."

"You have?" Denny said in surprise.

Janet nodded and gave him a warm smile. "I have something for you." From behind her back, she produced a large chocolate-covered doughnut sitting on a lacy white paper doily. "I just wanted to let you know how glad I am that you're—"

"Thanks, Janet," Denny said, taking the doughnut from her. "But I really ought to give this to Elizabeth." He held the doughnut out to Elizabeth. "Please accept this as a very small token of my appreciation."

Janet glared at Elizabeth, her face turning a scary shade of purple.

"No, thank you," Elizabeth said quickly before Janet had a chance to explode. "I couldn't eat a thing. Really."

It was the truth. The look on Janet's face was giving her a heavy feeling in the pit of her stomach. The last thing she needed right now was to be on Janet's bad side.

But Denny didn't seem to notice Janet's expression. "Oh, come on, Elizabeth," he said, wrapping the doughnut in a tissue. "I'll put it in your backpack in case you get hungry later."

With that, Denny turned his back on Janet, grabbed Elizabeth's elbow, and began steering her toward her homeroom.

Elizabeth didn't need to glance back to know that the look Janet was giving her was deadly.

Five

By the end of third period, Elizabeth was feeling a little better. Lots of people had congratulated her without making too big of a deal over her.

Amy had said she was going to write a story on the rescue for the *Sixers*, the official sixth-grade newspaper, and she promised to get all the facts straight.

"Now, please don't make me out to be some kind of supergirl," Elizabeth begged as they walked to their next class. "The important point to get across is that I was able to help someone because I took a lifesaving course. I didn't do anything that anyone else wouldn't have done."

"I promise I won't embarrass you by going on endlessly like Denny," Amy responded. "But don't forget—Maria and I were there too. And we didn't go plunging into the water. You did. Like it or not, you're a hero," she said with a smile.

Elizabeth couldn't help smiling back. "Well, I don't feel much like a hero. But I'll tell you one thing—it's nice to know I can deal with a crisis."

Just then, Mr. Bowman, Elizabeth's favorite teacher, came out of his classroom and paused beside her. "Congratulations, Elizabeth," he said solemnly. "I'm very proud of you." He extended his hand and formally shook Elizabeth's. "It's not every day I get to shake the hand of such a remarkable person."

His warm smile and handshake made Elizabeth feel great. Mr. Bowman didn't praise people often, so when he did, it meant a lot.

"See you in class," he said, nodding at Amy before disappearing down the hall.

Denny suddenly appeared at Elizabeth's side. "Anything I can do for you before your next class?" he asked eagerly.

"I really can't think of anything."

"Carry your books?"

"No, thanks, I've only got this one."

"Get you a soda?"

Elizabeth pressed her lips together. *Calm down*, she told herself. *It's only for a day or two.* "No, thank you," she said as politely as she could.

"OK," Denny said agreeably. "But if you need anything at all, you let me know. Was Mr. Bowman congratulating you?" he asked.

Elizabeth nodded. "He shook my hand and told

me I was a remarkable person," she said proudly.

Denny slapped his hand to his forehead. "A *handshake*. That's feeble. Elizabeth, I'm so glad you said that. It makes me realize how little recognition you're getting. You deserve a lot more than a handshake. You deserve a medal. And I'm going to make sure you get one. I'll go talk to Mr. Clark right now. Mr. Clark should present it to you himself," he murmured, heading toward the office. "In fact, we should have an assembly held in your honor."

"NO!" Elizabeth said, louder than she intended.

Denny turned around in surprise.

"Please, Denny. Don't bother Mr. Clark. I don't want an assembly in my honor," Elizabeth insisted. "And I don't want a medal. Really."

"And I present this medal," Mr. Clark said proudly, "to Elizabeth Wakefield for bravery, courage, and heroism in the face of danger."

The crowded auditorium burst into enthusiastic applause. It was Tuesday, and true to his word, Denny had gotten Mr. Clark to present Elizabeth a medal at an assembly held in her honor.

Elizabeth looked out across the sea of faces and saw Jessica, Amy, and Maria applauding enthusiastically in the front row.

They were smiling proudly, but Elizabeth couldn't help feeling a little foolish. Lots of people would have done what she did. Why did Denny and everybody else have to make such a huge deal about it?

Even Mr. Clark was caught up in the whole thing. She had tried to tell him yesterday that the medal and the assembly weren't necessary, but he'd really liked Denny's idea. "It's important to celebrate heroism," he had told her. "You've set a wonderful example for your peers."

Mr. Clark smiled broadly as he hung the little gold medal on a yellow ribbon around her neck.

The auditorium burst into applause again.

Denny sat in the front row and applauded in an exaggerated way, lifting his arms high up over his head.

Then he stood up and began urging others to do the same.

The applause grew louder as people all over the auditorium gave her a standing ovation.

Elizabeth smiled in thanks, but she knew her face was bright red with embarrassment. She took a deep breath. *I hope Denny's satisfied now,* she thought. *I can't take much more of this.*

"I'm not totally satisfied with that medal," Denny said, critically eyeing the little gold star. "It's kind of small. I'm going to ask Mr. Clark to find you a bigger one."

"No!" Elizabeth cried.

Denny blinked at her outburst, and his face took on an expression of hurt surprise. "Geez, Elizabeth. I'm just trying to show my gratitude."

Elizabeth felt guilty. She didn't want Denny to think she didn't appreciate what he had done—even though she didn't. "I mean . . . uhhhh . . . this medal is fine. A bigger one would be kind of heavy," she added quickly.

They were standing together in the cafeteria line—Denny had insisted on walking her to the cafeteria after the assembly.

Denny shrugged. "OK," he said happily. "I guess you're right. The medal's not bad. And the ribbon is pretty nice."

Elizabeth was only half listening to Denny as he talked. She was busy studying the menu.

Goulash. Rolls. Bread pudding. *Yuck!* she thought. She hated the cafeteria's goulash. Nobody knew exactly what was in it. Jessica said it was the leftovers from old science experiments. And the rolls they served with it were always mushy.

Too bad I didn't bring my lunch, she thought as she took a tray and began moving through the line with Denny following close behind her.

A cafeteria worker wearing a net over her red hair barely looked at her as she dropped a scoop of goulash on Elizabeth's plate.

"That's it?" Denny cried out in disgust. "That's all the goulash you're going to give her?" Denny shook his head at the cafeteria worker. "Maybe you don't realize this girl is the hero of Sweet Valley Middle School."

The cafeteria worker looked up from the vat of goulash and stared at Elizabeth. Then she blinked in surprise. "My goodness. That's right. I read about you in the paper last Saturday." The lady turned her head. "Hey, Gladys! Joe! Frances! This is the little girl who saved that boy at the beach on Friday."

The next thing Elizabeth knew, four white-uniformed cafeteria workers were peering intently at her over the high aluminum counter.

"Little thing, isn't she?" commented one lady.

"Hard to believe she swam out through ten-foot waves," said the man.

"Lots of sharks in that part of the water, I hear," one of the other ladies said.

"Looks like she could use a few more pounds," the redheaded lady with the hairnet said with a smile.

Plop!

Several long-handled spoons seemed to appear out of nowhere to pile food onto Elizabeth's plate.

"That's plenty," Elizabeth protested as they dropped one, two, three, *four* mushy rolls on her plate.

"But those rolls are tiny," Denny said, motioning toward Elizabeth's plate. Gladys grinned and dropped two more rolls on it.

Denny smiled at the cafeteria workers. "Gotta keep the hero of Sweet Valley Middle School ready for action, right?"

"Right!" the cafeteria workers echoed.

They had reached the end of the line now, and Elizabeth reached for her tray. But before she could pick it up, Denny whisked it away. "I'll carry it for you," he said. "And I'm going to sit right next to you to be sure you eat every bite."

Elizabeth sighed heavily. Great. Just what she needed.

"You know, I'll bet there *were* sharks out there in the ocean," Denny said thoughtfully as he carried her tray toward an empty table.

"I don't know about that—" Elizabeth began.

"I've heard about people spotting sharks in the area. We were out pretty far, you know," he went on.

"I really don't think—"

"I guess you were too busy saving me to notice the sharks," Denny said. He put her tray down on the table, then pulled her chair out for her.

"Denny," Elizabeth began, determined to correct him.

"I'll be right back," Denny said, interrupting her again. "I forgot my own tray."

Elizabeth stared sadly at her heaping plate. What a waste of food! One scoop of goulash was unappetizing enough. *Two* were gross. Elizabeth pushed the goulash to the side of her plate.

She looked up in time to see Todd Wilkins walking toward her with his tray. She felt truly happy for the first time all day. Todd wasn't Elizabeth's boyfriend, but they liked each other a lot. They had gone out together a few times, and Todd was the first boy Elizabeth ever kissed.

"Hi, Elizabeth," Todd said, pulling out a chair across from Elizabeth. "Is it OK if I—"

But before he could finish, Denny materialized again and took Todd's chair. "Sorry to leave you for so long," Denny said, giving Todd a warning look.

Todd frowned and took the seat next to Denny.

"Hope I'm not in the way," he said with a slight note of sarcasm.

"Of course not," Denny said quickly. "Elizabeth and I were just about to have lunch." Denny flashed her a big smile. "There's nobody I'd rather have lunch with."

Todd stood up and grabbed his tray. "Maybe I'd better sit someplace else."

Before Elizabeth could even open her mouth to protest, he was walking angrily away.

"Did you sign the petition?" Tamara asked the other girls at the Unicorner, the special table where the Unicorns always gathered for lunch.

"What petition?" Grace Oliver asked.

Tamara laughed. "The petition that Denny Jacobson is circulating. He wants Mr. Clark to designate an official *Elizabeth Wakefield Day*."

Mandy Miller laughed too. "Poor Denny's getting pretty carried away."

But Janet didn't seem to think it was funny at all. "That does it," she sputtered angrily. She turned toward Jessica. "I've had it with that publicity-grubbing sister of yours."

"Janet!" Jessica protested. "That's not fair. Elizabeth *did* save Denny's life, remember?"

"I'll bet the whole thing is a big exaggeration," Janet said scornfully. "She probably jumped into the water and swam after him just to make herself look good. Maybe she did it because she likes Denny."

"That's ridiculous, Janet," Mary Wallace said.

"Elizabeth would never do something like that."

"Mary's right," Mandy added.

Jessica felt a wave of relief. She was glad the other girls were defending Elizabeth too. She didn't want to have to take Janet on alone.

"We should all be really grateful to Elizabeth," Jessica said hotly. "And if you like Denny as much as you say, you should be the most grateful of all."

Janet lifted one eyebrow. "Is that so?"

"You bet," Jessica said.

"And it's fine with you that your sister's getting all the attention?"

"Sure," Jessica said. "She deserves it."

"Take a look over there," Janet said in a nasty voice, pointing over Jessica's shoulder.

All the girls turned to look. Jessica's eyes flew open in surprise.

Aaron Dallas, Jessica's sort-of boyfriend, was sitting next to Elizabeth, hanging on every word she said. His excited voice could be heard all the way across the lunchroom.

"What about the lightning?" Aaron asked breathlessly. "Were you worried about being electrocuted?"

Jessica felt like kicking herself. She'd told Aaron an exaggerated version of the rescue to impress him. Maybe she'd gone one step too far. *Why didn't I keep my big mouth shut?* she wondered miserably.

Six

Elizabeth tossed in her bed, twisting and turning, tangling herself up in the sheets.

The waves were pounding all around her. She was swimming as hard as she could, but the shore kept moving farther and farther away.

Amy and Maria were standing at the water's edge, waving their arms to encourage her, but the current was pulling her out to sea, and Amy and Maria were getting smaller and smaller.

There was a terrible clap of thunder, and a bolt of lightning split the sky, illuminating the dark waters. Elizabeth caught a glimpse of a fin moving toward her.

"Oh no!" she shrieked. "It's a shark!"

Elizabeth tightened her grasp on Denny and began to swim even harder. Behind her, she could feel the ocean swell.

"Nooooo!" she cried again as an enormous wave broke over her head, washing Denny away and sending her tumbling through the water, head over heels. "Help! Help!"

She jerked her body as hard as she could, trying to break the grip of the current.

"Oh!" Elizabeth cried as she tumbled off the bed and hit the floor with a hard thump. She sat up, breathing hard and blinking in confusion as the dream receded and her head cleared. *What an awful, awful dream*, she thought.

"That does it," she said out loud. She got up, straightened out her blankets, and crawled back into bed. "Denny can walk me to school tomorrow, but it's the last time."

Denny Jacobson was taking over her days, and now he was ruining her nights. She'd never stop having these dreams until he and everybody else quit talking about the rescue all the time.

"I'm through with being a hero," she said firmly. Then she turned out the light and lay back down— determined not to dream about tidal waves, lightning, or sharks ever again.

"What are you doing?" a voice whispered.

Elizabeth screamed in surprise. She twirled around and saw Amy rear back and stare at her with wide eyes.

"What's the matter with you?" Amy exclaimed.

"Why did you sneak up on me like that?" Elizabeth demanded.

"I didn't sneak up on you," Amy said defensively. "I just wanted to know what you were doing." She began to giggle. "You looked like you were hiding."

Elizabeth blushed. She *had* been hiding—she was standing behind the bank of lockers, peeking around the corner. But she hadn't realized it looked so obvious.

"OK, I am hiding from somebody," she admitted with an embarrassed smile.

"Who?"

Elizabeth quickly looked right and left to make sure nobody was near enough to hear their conversation. She took Amy's arm and pulled her farther back behind the lockers where they couldn't be seen. "I'm hiding from Denny," she whispered.

"Why?"

"Because he's driving me *crazy*," Elizabeth said through gritted teeth. "This hero-worship thing is getting totally out of hand. I can't take two steps without Denny following me, or offering to do something for me, or telling somebody that I'm a hero. It's embarrassing. It's sickening. It's exhausting. And it's . . . *irritating*."

"Geez," Amy said. "I didn't realize it was that bad. Have you told Denny?"

Elizabeth moaned. "How can I? I don't want to hurt his feelings."

Amy nodded. "He *has* gotten a little carried away," she said, trying to suppress a giggle. "Lots of people have noticed that he's kind of obsessed with you. It's like he has a crush on you that's getting bigger every day."

Elizabeth shook her head miserably. "Unfortunately, one of the people who's noticed is Todd. Every time he's tried to talk to me, Denny interrupts us and takes over the conversation."

"What are you going to do?"

"My mother says I'm just going to have to wait it out and hope he gets over it," Elizabeth replied. "So I'm waiting. And hiding."

She stepped out cautiously from behind the lockers. "Well, it looks like the coast is clear. I'm going to make a run for it."

"Good luck," Amy said.

Elizabeth stepped out into the hallway and began hurrying toward the door at the end of the hall that led outside. If she could just make it out the door and into the street, she could take the long way home—past the square and around Garden Street. Denny would never think of looking for her over there.

She was running now. The door was getting closer. She was almost home free.

"Elizabeth!" Denny yelled, stepping out of the boys' bathroom. "There you are. I've been looking for you since first period."

Oh no. Elizabeth's heart sank. Still, she forced herself to smile. "Hi, Denny."

"Ready to go home? Here, give me your backpack. Not that you can't handle it. A girl who can swim through twenty-foot waves in shark-infested water during an electrical storm can obviously carry her own backpack," Denny said.

Oh, brother. Elizabeth knew Denny was trying to make her feel good, but it was having the opposite effect.

"You're right," Elizabeth said, stepping back and clutching her backpack close to her chest. "I'll carry it. And you don't need to walk me home. Really."

"Come on, Elizabeth. Do you really think I'd let you walk home alone lugging all those books after you saved my life? What kind of person do you think I am?"

Denny reached over and put his hand on the strap of her backpack.

But Elizabeth pulled it back. "Don't you have anything better to do than follow me around?" she snapped, her patience finally giving out.

Denny's face fell and his eyes widened in disbelief.

Elizabeth immediately regretted losing her temper. "What I mean is, uh . . . I'm sure there are things you'd rather be doing than carrying my books home. And I wouldn't want to take you away from them."

Denny smiled. "There's nothing more important to me than letting you know how grateful I am to you— and how special I think you are."

With that, Denny snatched the backpack from Elizabeth's grasp. The move was so sudden that Elizabeth stumbled backward and fell down hard on her seat.

She sat there stunned, but Denny didn't even notice. He was already heading out the door with her backpack. "Let's take the long way home," he was saying. "Past the square and around Garden Street. That will give us more time to talk."

"Your sister makes me want to puke," Janet said. "I can't believe she's leading Denny around like this."

Jessica sighed. "My parents say it's a phase," she assured Janet. "They think Denny will get over it in a couple of days." Jessica was standing with Janet at the other end of the hall, and they had just watched Elizabeth and Denny leaving together.

Janet turned toward Jessica and gave her a haughty look. "Well, I'm going through a phase too. My sick-of-hearing-about-Elizabeth-Wakefield phase. She's making the Unicorns look bad."

"What do you mean?" Jessica asked.

"She's always bragging and acting like she's better than we are," Janet insisted.

"But—"

"I'm sick of it. And if you don't figure out some way of making her stop it and leave Denny alone, you can forget about being a hostess at the fair."

"Janet!" Jessica cried. "That's so un—"

"One of the duties of a Unicorn is being loyal to the other members—especially senior ones. It wouldn't be fair for me to ask you to be a hostess at the Teen Health Fair when there are other members of the club who deserve it more."

"But Janet—" Jessica began.

Janet shook her head. "Don't *but Janet* me," she hissed. "Just do something. Or else!"

*   *   *

"Janet is making my life miserable!" Jessica shouted in frustration as she barged into Elizabeth's room that afternoon. "This thing with Denny has gotten completely out of hand."

"You're telling me!" Elizabeth shouted back. "You can tell Janet that I'm as sick of having Denny following me around as she is. He's driving me insane!" Elizabeth threw down her notebook, stood up, and stormed over to the window. "Look down there," she ordered, yanking the curtains aside.

Jessica stepped over to the window and looked out. "What am I looking at?"

"Over there, by the oak tree."

"Denny!" Jessica exclaimed.

"You got it."

"What's he doing?" Jessica asked uneasily.

"He's decided that walking me to school isn't enough," Elizabeth groaned. "So he's waiting for me to come out and ask him to do something. I wonder if he'll ever go home, or if he plans on sleeping out there. He's got to get hungry at some point."

"Wow!" Jessica exclaimed. "He's really gone overboard with this hero-worship stuff, hasn't he?"

Elizabeth dropped her head in her hands. "I feel like he's stalking me."

"It *is* kind of creepy," Jessica agreed. "But there must be something you can do about it."

"What?" Elizabeth squeaked.

Jessica peered out the window again, then she

stepped behind the curtain as Denny's face lifted toward Elizabeth's window. "I've got an idea."

"Tell me," Elizabeth said. "Please."

Jessica tapped her finger thoughtfully against her chin. "Maybe if Denny became a hero himself, it would cure him of worshiping you."

Elizabeth frowned. "What do you mean?"

Jessica's eyes sparkled with excitement, the way they always did when she was formulating a plan. "Here's what I think we should do. . . ."

"Steven Wakefield, you are the most conceited guy I've ever met!" Cathy said angrily.

"I am *not* conceited," Steven protested.

"You are too. You've been bragging for the last half hour about hitting eight shots at practice—and you haven't said one word about my making *ten*."

"You made ten baskets?" Steven exclaimed in surprise as he shut his locker. "Why didn't you tell me?"

It was late in the afternoon, and Steven had just come from the gym after basketball practice. Cathy had had practice too. The two of them almost always went out for a soda afterward.

"I *did* tell you," Cathy insisted. "I've told you three times. But you've been so busy bragging about being a basketball star that you didn't listen."

"Well, I *am* a basketball star," Steven said with a grin. "Look at this."

Steven proudly showed her the newspaper that one of his teammates had given him. It was a copy of

The Oracle, Sweet Valley High's newspaper. It was opened to the sports page and folded back to reveal a headline that read "Steven Wakefield Saves the Day."

He stood up straighter and puffed out his chest as Cathy's eyes quickly scanned the article beneath the headline. "It's a story about the last game," he said. "Guess you feel pretty lucky to be dating somebody like me, huh?"

Cathy shoved the paper back into his hands, grabbed her books out of her locker, and shut it with a bang. "That does it, Steven. I'm not talking to you until you get over yourself. Good-bye!"

Steven watched her hurry down the hall with his mouth open and his heart beating angrily. He couldn't believe how unreasonable she was being. Why shouldn't he be proud of himself? He was one of the best players on the team. Maybe the best. At this rate, he'd be captain of the team next year, while he was still only a sophomore.

He frowned. Fine! If Cathy was ready to throw away a potential captain of the basketball team, that was her problem. There were lots of other girls who would love to hear about his last game, and how many points he had scored in practice today.

Girls like Pam Martin.

Steven smiled, thinking about Pam. She was new, and he'd hardly had a chance to talk to her. But he thought she was pretty. Very pretty.

"Hey, Wakefield. Wake up. You look like you're

falling asleep." Steven looked up and grinned at his best friend, Joe Howell.

Like Steven, Joe was a freshman. He was also Janet Howell's older brother.

"Want to walk home together?" Joe asked, hoisting his backpack over his shoulder.

"Sure," Steven said quickly. "It's not like anybody else wants to walk home with me."

"What does that mean?" Joe asked.

"I just had a fight with Cathy."

"Too bad," Joe said. "Cathy's great."

"I'm not sure she's *so* great. In fact, I'm thinking it might be time to get out and play the field a little."

"Play the field!" Joe laughed. "You can't be serious. With who?"

"Pam Martin."

"That new girl?"

Steven nodded.

"She is pretty cute," Joe agreed. "I don't know her very well."

"Me neither," Steven smiled. "But I'd like to. And I wouldn't be surprised if she'd like to get to know me, too." He pointed to the article in the paper. "After all, I am a big basketball star."

Joe's eyebrows shot up. "Is that right?"

"Sure," Steven said, breathing on his nails and pretending to polish them on the front of his shirt. "I'm definitely the fastest guy on the team."

A little crooked smile played across Joe's face. "Well, here's your chance to impress her, *Star*."

Steven quickly turned. Pam Martin was walking in their direction. She had long, reddish-blond hair and wore round wire-rimmed glasses. In her arms she carried a stack of trigonometry books.

Steven gulped nervously and felt his self-confidence fade a little. On second thought, maybe going after Pam Martin wasn't such a great idea. "I don't know," Steven said in an uneasy voice. "Look at those books. If she's taking trig already, she must be pretty brainy. I'm not too good in math. She'd probably think I was a dumb jock."

"Come on, Steven," Joe argued. "Go talk to her."

"I don't think so," Steven said.

"Go *on*," Joe urged.

Before Steven could think of a better excuse, he felt Joe plant his hand between his shoulder blades and shove.

"Yeow!" he cried as he careened down the hallway, stumbled over his feet, and sprawled on the linoleum floor directly in Pam's path.

"Yikes!" Pam shrieked as she tripped over Steven and fell on top of him.

Her glasses flew off and skittered across the hall floor, and her heavy textbooks flew in all directions.

"I'm sorry," Steven sputtered, trying to scramble to his feet and collect her books at the same time. "That was an accident. I don't know how it happened. I was just telling my friend how I would like to meet you, and . . ."

Pam gave him a frosty look and rolled her eyes. "So

you thought this was a good way of meeting me?"

"No," Steven protested. "It's just that my friend . . ."

Steven looked around, hoping Joe would jump in and explain. But Joe seemed to have disappeared. He felt himself blushing furiously. Now he looked like a total fool. Like some geek who hung out in the halls by himself, tripping girls to get their attention.

"You're a little old to have an imaginary friend," she said. "But the next time you and your imaginary friend are goofing around, please try not to plow into me." She climbed to her feet.

Steven wet his lips nervously. This wasn't going the way he'd expected. In his mind, he'd pictured himself sweeping her off her feet. Totally impressing her with his basketball achievements. But she wasn't impressed at all. She was impatient and irritated.

"Have you seen my glasses?" she asked.

"Excuse me," a voice said calmly. "Are these yours?"

Steven looked up in surprise. Joe had appeared—as if he were just arriving on the scene—and was holding out a pair of wire-rimmed glasses.

"I just found them on the floor," Joe explained.

Pam took the glasses and put them on. She blinked her eyes, focusing on Joe. Then she broke into a smile. "Thank you," she said in a friendly voice. "I'd be lost without my glasses."

Steven darted a nasty look at Joe. What was his supposed friend trying to pull?

"You're very welcome," Joe said in a deep and phony-sounding voice. Then he returned Steven's glare with a bland smile. "Hello, Steven." He turned his attention back to Pam. "I'm Joe Howell, by the way."

"Nice to meet you, Joe. I'm Pam Martin."

"And I'm Steven Wakefield," Steven said, stepping in front of Joe.

Pam Martin's eyebrows drew together over the bridge of her nose. "Wakefield. Wakefield. Hmm. That name sounds really familiar."

"I'm on the basketball team," Steven said proudly. "Maybe that's why."

"Nooooo," Pam said thoughtfully. "I don't think that's it."

"I also play first trombone in the student orchestra," he added. "Maybe you've heard somebody mention my . . . uh . . . musical ability?"

"Noooo . . ." Pam mused.

Suddenly she snapped her fingers. "Wakefield is the name I saw in the Sweet Valley High paper today."

"That's right," Steven agreed. He pulled out the newspaper again. "See. That's me."

Pam nodded absently. "That's not what I was talking about." Quickly she took the paper and opened it to the front page. "That's what I was talking about. Wakefield is the name of the girl who saved that boy from drowning."

Steven's eyes widened. Smiling up at him from the front page of the paper was his very own sister, Elizabeth. The Sweet Valley High paper had reprinted the article that had appeared in the weekend paper.

"Any relation to you?" Pam asked.

"My sister," Steven answered.

"That's what I call a real hero," Pam said briskly. She handed Steven back the paper and then turned to face Joe. "I guess I'll see you tomorrow," she said with a smile. "Thanks for finding my glasses. See you."

"See you," Joe and Steven both answered as Pam hurried away.

"Looks like Pam Martin is more impressed with Elizabeth than she is with you," Joe teased as soon as Pam was out of earshot.

"I can't believe this!" Steven yelped. "How could you pull something like that? You made me look like a total bozo."

Joe grinned. "I think Pam Martin is cute too. So why shouldn't I get to know her?"

"Because I like her, and I'm your best friend," Steven reminded him.

"That didn't stop you from asking Jill Hale out a while back," Joe said.

"You weren't interested in Jill Hale," Steven argued.

"But you didn't know that at the time," Joe insisted stubbornly.

Jill Hale was a girl that Steven had had an enormous crush on a few months ago. He'd even tried to win her away from Joe. As it turned out, Jill wasn't the right girl for either one of them. She'd turned out to be kind of a snob. That's when Steven had realized the girl he really liked was Cathy.

"So what's your point?" Steven asked with a scowl.

"My point is that all's fair in love and war," Joe said, grinning at Steven.

Steven's frown relaxed and he grinned back. "May the best man win," he said genially, extending his hand.

Joe took Steven's hand and shook it. "May the best man win," he echoed.

"There's a party at the Pool Club on Friday after school," Steven said. "Will you be there?"

"Will you?" Joe asked quickly.

"You bet." Steven laughed. "Pam is going to be there. So I'll be watching your every move."

Seven

"This plan is perfect," Jessica said as she and Elizabeth pedaled their bikes toward the Sweet Valley Pool Club.

"If you say so," Elizabeth said doubtfully. "I just hope it works."

"Are you kidding? It's got to work," Jessica insisted. "It's brilliant."

"It's also crazy," Elizabeth pointed out.

"Of course it is," Jessica agreed. "*I* thought it up."

"That's what's worrying me," Elizabeth said.

"Ha ha," Jessica said dryly. "You know my plans always work out for the best."

"Things always work out for the best *in spite* of your plans," Elizabeth countered with a giggle.

Jessica was always formulating harebrained schemes to get the two of them in or out of some kind of trouble. And Elizabeth was always trying not to get involved. But somehow Jessica almost always managed to mix her up in them, no matter how crazy her schemes were.

"Trust me," Jessica said. "By the end of the afternoon, Denny will be cured of his hero worship. He'll quit following you around and driving you crazy. And Janet won't have any reason to be jealous anymore. Which means she'll let me be a hostess at the Teen Health Fair. Two problems solved with one brilliant plan."

"And once Denny is acting normal," Elizabeth added in a hopeful voice, "maybe everybody else will too. Did you know Randy Mason actually asked me to autograph my picture today—the one that was in the paper?"

Jessica began to laugh. "I wish somebody would ask me for my autograph. I think it would be great to be famous and have my picture in the paper."

"Oh yeah? Well, somebody else cut out that same picture, drew a mustache on it, and slipped it through the vents of my locker with 'You phony' written on it."

"You're kidding!" Jessica exclaimed. Then she frowned. "I'll bet it was Janet."

"Believe me. Being a hero is not all it's cracked up to be. People either gush all over you, or they get jealous and resent you. Neither way is fun."

"Well, after this afternoon, Sweet Valley will have a new hero," Jessica assured her. "You did tell Denny to meet us here, didn't you?"

Elizabeth nodded. "He said he'd hurry over as soon as he changed into his bathing suit."

"Perfect," Jessica said happily.

It was a gorgeous day. When the twins pulled up to the Pool Club, they saw lots of cars and bikes.

"Looks like everybody's in the mood to swim today," Elizabeth said nervously. "Maybe we should try this another time. I'm probably going to wind up looking like an idiot, and I'd rather not look like an idiot in front of the whole school."

"Fine," Jessica said cheerfully, climbing off of her bicycle and locking it to the rack. "Forget it. Spend the rest of your life eating triple portions of goulash. See if I care."

"All right, all right," Elizabeth said hastily, climbing off her bike.

"Looks like Steven's here," Jessica said, pointing to a familiar bike.

"And a lot of other people from Sweet Valley High," Elizabeth said as they opened the gate that led to the pool area and walked in. She wished they weren't. It was going to be bad enough looking ridiculous in front of people her own age, let alone high-school kids.

There were a few people in the pool, but most of the kids were sitting around the tables on the grass, eating big plates of food.

Big speakers were set up all around the patio, and loud rock and roll blasted out over the pool area.

"Good thing the snack bar is open," Elizabeth said.

"What?" Jessica asked, cupping her hand behind her ear.

"Good thing the snack bar is open!" Elizabeth repeated.

Jessica nodded. "Right. Come on. Let's get some food."

"Did you say *two* submarine sandwiches?" the man behind the counter asked in surprise.

Elizabeth nodded. "That's right!" she shouted over the loud music.

The man pushed his white paper hat farther back on his head and gave Jessica and Elizabeth a curious look. "They're pretty big, you know. Most people split one."

Elizabeth nodded. "I know. But we're very hungry."

Just then, she felt Jessica nudge her in the ribs. "Here he comes."

Elizabeth looked over and saw Denny hurrying toward her. He was wearing his bathing suit and a T-shirt. His towel was slung over his shoulder.

"Hi!" he said with a smile as he joined the girls. "Elizabeth, you should have let me get those for you," he chided, looking at the sandwiches.

"That's OK, Denny. But you *can* carry them." Elizabeth handed him the tray that the man at the counter had just shoved in her direction.

"I thought we were going to swim," Denny said.

"Oh, we'll swim," Elizabeth assured him. "But I need to eat first. Come on. Let's get a table for three."

*   *   *

"Aren't you going to eat your sandwich?" Elizabeth asked Jessica.

"I guess I'm not very hungry after all," Jessica said. "Do you want it?"

"Don't you think you should go easy if you're planning to swim?" Denny asked Elizabeth uneasily. "You're not really supposed to swim after you've eaten. And you've already eaten one huge sandwich."

"I'll . . . oommpph . . . be . . . fine . . ." Elizabeth insisted through a mouthful of sandwich. She chewed vigorously, then reached for her soda and took a long sip. "That stuff about not eating before you swim is just an old wives' tale."

Jessica lifted her hand to her face to hide her smile. Elizabeth was playing her part beautifully. When she got in the water and pretended to have a cramp, Denny would be sure to believe it was real after watching her put away all that food.

Denny frowned. "I'm not so sure you're right about that. All my life people have warned me against eating before going into the water."

Elizabeth reached for another half a sandwich. "Oh, well." She laughed. "I'm not worried."

"You aren't? Really? Well, maybe you're right. If there's one person I trust, Elizabeth, it's you. Maybe it *is* an old wives' tale. Say, those sandwiches look good. I think I'll go get one too."

Fifteen minutes later, Jessica crouched behind the

large potted plant that stood beside the white stucco wall of the poolhouse. She peeked around the plant and watched Elizabeth bob around in the water. The music was blasting even louder now, and a lot of people were dancing on the grass, several yards away from the pool.

Steven stood directly under one of the loudspeakers, talking to Joe and a girl with reddish-blond hair whom Jessica had never seen before.

Denny lay on a lounge chair close to the pool, with a magazine spread over his face.

Jessica inspected the lifeguard stand. The woman sitting in the tall, ladder-backed chair was a new lifeguard. Neither Elizabeth nor Jessica had ever seen her before.

Ah ha, Jessica thought happily as the lifeguard climbed down and walked past her, disappearing into the ladies' locker room. *Here's our chance.*

She put her fingers to her lips and whistled the signal to Elizabeth. Elizabeth nodded slightly, then swam out into the deeper water.

"Help!" Elizabeth shouted, her voice just barely audible over the music. "Help!"

Jessica watched Denny eagerly, waiting for him to jump up and race to the rescue. But he didn't move. He just lay there like a beached whale.

"*Help!*" Elizabeth shouted. "Help! I've got a cramp!"

Still Denny didn't move. Jessica figured he had to be alive, because his chest was rising up and down. This was unbelievable! Denny was *asleep*. Probably because he had also eaten two submarine sand-wiches, Jessica thought.

Jessica picked up a small piece of gravel and lobbed it in Denny's direction. But she missed. The piece of gravel sailed harmlessly over his legs.

A couple of people were beginning to look over toward the pool, trying to figure out if somebody really was in trouble, or just fooling around.

Wake up, Denny, Jessica prayed. *Hurry.*

Elizabeth splashed dramatically, then disappeared beneath the surface. A few bubbles floated to the top.

"Arrggggg!" Jessica groaned out loud. There was no way around it. If they wanted Denny to save Elizabeth, Jessica was going to have to run over there and give him a good, hard shake. She crept out from behind the potted plant and started hurrying to Denny, when suddenly a small figure came running past her, hurtling toward the water like a cannonball.

Blub! Blub! Blub!

Elizabeth floated around at the bottom of the pool, letting out a few air bubbles now and then for effect. She was really hoping Denny would get the idea fast, because she couldn't stay down here long.

Suddenly a familiar face appeared in front of hers.

"*Amy!*" she cried. Because she was underwater, no sound came out of her mouth, just a bunch of air bubbles.

The next thing she knew, Amy was wrapping her arm around her neck and yanking her upward.

Elizabeth tried to struggle, but Amy tightened her grasp and pulled even harder. Elizabeth let her body relax. There was no sense in fighting it. Amy thought she was drowning and was obviously determined to save her.

The water made an explosive noise when Amy and Elizabeth broke the surface. Amy was determinedly towing her to the side of the pool.

Elizabeth hissed. "Cut it out."

Amy gasped. "Elizabeth! Are you all right?"

Elizabeth took Amy's arm from around her neck and glared at her. "Yes, I'm all right. Now, would you please go away?"

"But I thought . . . I heard you yell for help . . . I saw you sink . . ." Amy coughed up some water and took a deep breath. "You scared me to death," she finished angrily.

Elizabeth looked over and saw Denny still sleeping on the lounge chair, his magazine still over his face. Jessica was standing behind him, looking sheepish.

"I'm sorry, Amy," Elizabeth said with a sigh, swimming toward the side of the pool.

"Hey!" a voice barked.

Elizabeth and Amy looked up and saw the lifeguard glaring at them. She had a thick layer of white goo spread over her nose and a whistle around her neck. It made her look very authoritative. "Is there some trouble here?" she demanded.

"N—no," Elizabeth managed.

"No," Amy echoed.

"Somebody said they saw you calling for help," the lifeguard persisted. "Were you?"

"Well . . . sort of . . ." Elizabeth said softly. Her cheeks were red with embarrassment. A few kids had turned to stare at them, and Elizabeth knew it was obvious that she was getting in trouble.

The lifeguard fixed Elizabeth with an angry stare. "Did your parents ever tell you the story of the boy who cried wolf?" she asked.

"Yes," Elizabeth said meekly.

"I don't like people who cry wolf in my pool," the lifeguard continued. "Don't leave the pool area," she ordered. "I'm going to talk to the manager about this." Then she turned and stalked off toward the office.

Jessica threw up her arms in frustration. "So it wasn't a complete success."

Elizabeth rolled her eyes. "It wasn't a *complete success*? Jessica! It backfired completely. And furthermore, I got yelled at by the lifeguard. This is the last time I'm listening to you."

"Fine," Jessica retorted. "From now on, you can come up with your own plans. I'm going to get something to drink."

Fuming, Jessica hurried toward the refreshment stand. So her plan hadn't been quite as brilliant as she'd thought. But it was mostly Denny's fault. How dare he fall asleep? She cast a last look over her shoulder and saw him still stretched out, peacefully napping in the sun.

Jessica jumped as a deep voice addressed her. "Young lady, would you please come into the office?"

Jessica looked up and saw the manager of the pool standing in the door of his office and gesturing to her. She swallowed. The only people who got called into the manager's office were people who were in some kind of trouble.

Jessica walked hesitantly into the office.

"Is this the girl?" the manager asked.

That's when Jessica noticed the lifeguard standing in the back of the office. The lifeguard nodded. "That's her."

The manager frowned at Jessica. "Young lady, people who pretend to be in trouble in the water when they're not are playing a very dangerous and foolish game."

Jessica sucked in her breath with a gasp. So *that's* why they had called her in. They thought she was Elizabeth.

"But I . . ."

The manager held up his hand. "Let me finish, please." He launched into a long lecture on water safety while the lifeguard nodded after every point he made.

Jessica forced herself to look interested in what the manager was saying, but it was too incredibly boring. After a while, she started watching the action in the pool area through the big plate-glass window behind the manager's desk.

She saw Denny finally sit up. He yawned, hauled

himself out of his chair, and walked toward the water, testing the temperature with his toe.

Nobody else was swimming. All the other kids were dancing on the lawn, lining up for the snack bar, or, like Steven, flirting under the loudspeakers.

Denny stretched one last time, raising his arms high in the air, and then he leaned forward and dove into the pool, making a big splash.

"I get it," Amy said as she and Elizabeth came out of the women's locker room. "That was a great idea. I'm sorry I messed up your plan."

"That's OK," Elizabeth said dejectedly. "I guess I might as well find Jessica, wake Denny up, and go home. It's been kind of a long afternoon." She looked toward the lounge chairs. "Where is he, anyway?"

"He's over there," Amy said, pointing toward the deep end of the pool.

Elizabeth looked over at the pool and saw Denny bobbing awkwardly. There was something strange about the way he was swimming—his movements were sort of jerky. And his face was contorted and white.

"Oh my gosh," Elizabeth gasped. "He looks like he's in trouble."

She looked around quickly for the lifeguard, but the tall chair with the umbrella at the top was empty.

She looked for Steven. But he was yards away, and his back was turned to her. He was right under a loudspeaker too. He'd never hear her yelling for him.

Elizabeth was still trying to figure out what to do when suddenly Denny disappeared under the surface, leaving only a trail of bubbles floating along the water. *No. It can't be*, she thought desperately.

"Denny!" she screamed, running toward the pool and diving in headfirst.

Eight

◇

"I'm on the baseball team," Joe said proudly.

"Oh, really?" Pam said, her voice rising with interest. "I love baseball. I think it's a great sport. I was on the softball team at my old school."

Steven stood there, clenching his fists. Joe Howell was supposed to be his best friend, but he was turning out to be a traitor. A back-stabber.

Steven had approached Pam and started a conversation. Then Joe had come along and taken over. After that, Pam hadn't said two words to Steven. In fact, every time he said something, she gave him a blank look, as if she were making an effort to be polite but wished he would just go away.

He had the uncomfortable feeling that she saw him as an immature kid, somebody who tripped people in the halls for fun.

Pam smiled at Joe. "I'm going to get something to drink. I'll see you later."

"See you," Joe said.

"See you," Steven echoed.

As soon as she was gone, Steven grabbed Joe's arm. "Maybe you don't realize it, but you're getting in the way every time I try to have a conversation with her."

"So?"

"So how about giving me a break and letting me talk to her for a while?"

Joe grinned. "Why should I?"

"I'll do your English homework for a week," Steven offered.

"Forget it," Joe said with a laugh.

"Unbelievable!" they heard a voice shout.

Steven and Joe looked over toward the pool.

"What's going on?" Joe asked a boy who came running past them.

"Elizabeth Wakefield just saved Denny Jacobson," he said in a breathless voice. "*Again!*"

"Thank you, Elizabeth," Denny gasped. "I don't know what to say." He'd been lying on the concrete that surrounded the pool ever since Elizabeth hauled him out of the pool.

"What happened?" the lifeguard demanded as she and the manager pushed their way through the crowd toward Denny and Elizabeth.

"I got this terrible cramp," Denny explained. He

pointed to his side. "Right here. It was so painful I couldn't swim anymore."

The lifeguard frowned. "Didn't I see you eating a huge submarine sandwich a little while ago?"

Denny nodded.

"That certainly explains what happened," the lifeguard said. "I hope you've learned a lesson from this. Eating heavily before a swim can be very dangerous."

"Thank you for saving me, Elizabeth," Denny said, reaching out and squeezing her hand. "I don't know what I would have done if you hadn't been there."

"Oh, don't thank me," Elizabeth begged. "If it hadn't been for me, you never would have eaten all those sandwiches and then gone swimming. In fact, it was all my fault that you got the cramp."

She caught a glimpse of Janet's scowling face in the crowd. "If I were you and you were me, I'd hate you . . . I mean . . . you'd hate me . . . I mean . . . you shouldn't like me anymore . . ."

Denny took Elizabeth's hand. "Not like you anymore? Are you kidding? Elizabeth, you're not just a hero, you're practically my *guardian angel*."

"I think I'm going to throw up," Joe said to Steven under his breath.

"That makes two of us," Steven whispered back. He stared at the scene before him. Elizabeth was kneeling by Denny, who lay flat on his back by the side of the pool. She was holding his hand.

"This is just about the worst thing that could have happened," Joe said.

Steven looked at his friend in surprise.

"Don't get me wrong. I'm glad Denny's safe," Joe said quickly. "I just wish somebody besides Elizabeth had saved him."

"*You* wish?" Steven said. "Denny practically lives at our house. You can't take a step without falling over him. He's constantly watching Elizabeth with a goofy expression. But I don't get it—why do *you* care what happens to Denny and Elizabeth?"

Joe shook his head and groaned. "Ever since this thing with Elizabeth and Denny started, Janet's been a nightmare to live with. She's jealous. And when Janet's not happy, she makes everybody else in the family miserable—me especially. Things got really tense around my house last night. Would you believe I went out to the garage and hid inside a giant tooth?"

Steven laughed. He'd heard Jessica talking about the tooth costume. "Too bad you didn't wear it today. I would've had a better chance with Pam."

"Unlikely, Wakefield," Joe shot back, giving Steven a slap on the back.

"Can't somebody do something?" Steven shouted from his bedroom later that evening.

"Alice," Mr. Wakefield yelled from the downstairs den. "Would you please tell that boy I'm trying to work?"

"Now, Ned," Elizabeth heard her mother respond.

"Just be patient. He'll go away when he gets tired."

"I wouldn't count on it," Jessica shouted from the top of the stairs. "He sounds like he's just getting warmed up."

"Maybe he'll go away when it gets dark," Mrs. Wakefield said hopefully.

Plink. Plink. Plink.

Denny plucked the strings of his out-of-tune guitar. "What would I dooooooooooo," he sang in a warbling voice, "without yoooouuuu?"

"Arrrggggg!" Elizabeth groaned, pulling her pillow over her head. "I don't know how much more of this I can stand."

Denny had spent the last hour standing underneath her window *serenading* her. She couldn't believe it. And to top it off, his voice was awful.

". . . my hero is braaaaaave . . . my hero is truuuu-uee . . ." Denny sang, strumming his guitar.

". . . and she's a good swimmer toooooooooo," he warbled. His voice rose on the last note and cracked.

Elizabeth reached over and turned on her radio, trying to block the sound.

"This is too much," Steven commented.

"Totally unbelievable," Jessica agreed.

Elizabeth sat up on her bed. Her brother and sister were both standing in the doorway.

"If he doesn't stop that, I'm going to lose my mind!" Elizabeth shrieked.

Steven and Jessica took a step backward in surprise. Elizabeth almost never got really angry.

Jessica gave her a sympathetic look. "I'm sorry, Lizzie," Jessica said. "I really thought my plan would work. But obviously it just made things worse. Who would have thought you would wind up saving Denny *again*?"

"It's like some kind of curse," Steven said. "It's like you're doomed to save him over and over again."

"I saw a horror movie like that once," Jessica added.

". . . my hero's on the honor roll . . . my hero has a heart of gold . . ."

Plink plink plink.

"That's the worst song I've ever heard," Steven said with a grimace. "He must be making it up as he goes along." He started to laugh. "I wonder if he takes requests."

"See if he knows any Johnny Buck," Jessica joked.

Steven started toward the window. "I'm going to ask for . . ."

Whap!

"Hey!" Steven cried as Elizabeth's pillow hit him squarely on the back.

"Don't you dare laugh," Elizabeth fumed. "If you'd been paying attention this afternoon instead of flirting with that girl, you might have seen what was going on, and then *you* could have saved Denny."

Steven grinned. "I wish I had. If you guys had just told me about your plan sooner, I *would* have saved Denny. That girl I was flirting with thinks I'm a bozo. It would have been nice to have her think I was a hero."

"Oh, who cares if she thinks you're a hero," Jessica muttered grumpily. "The person we were trying to make a hero out of was Denny."

Plink. Plink.

". . . My hero's name is Lizzie. She's really smart, not dizzy . . ."

Steven rubbed his hand thoughtfully over his chin. "Maybe there's more than one way to make Denny look like a hero. I think I might just have a brilliant idea."

Elizabeth and Jessica exchanged a look.

"If it involves water, forget it," Elizabeth said warily.

"What if Denny saved you from a mugger?" Steven suggested with a grin. "That would make him feel pretty heroic, wouldn't it?"

"I guess it would," Elizabeth agreed. "But who would try to mug me in Sweet Valley?"

"Joe Howell," Steven replied.

"So I pretend to be a mugger?"

"Right," Steven said into the telephone.

"And I pretend to mug Denny and Elizabeth after school tomorrow?"

"Right."

"Denny will try to protect Elizabeth, start yelling at me to go away. And then I run, like I'm really scared of him."

"Exactly," Steven responded. "That way Denny will feel like a hero himself, and he'll stop hanging around Elizabeth like a lost dog."

"Then Janet won't have to be jealous of Elizabeth anymore," Joe said excitedly. "Which means she'll stop making my life miserable. You wouldn't believe how nasty she's been since Elizabeth pulled Denny out of the pool this afternoon. I told her to get a life, and she didn't take it too well. Get this. She went through my book bag until she found a quiz that I flunked, and then she took it and showed it to my dad."

"Wow!" Steven breathed. "That's cruel."

"My dad was already in a horrible mood because of that giant tooth that's in our garage. It's taking up so much room he can't get his car in there and he's had to park it on the street. He totally lost it."

"Your house sounds even worse than mine," Steven said sympathetically.

"Which actually gives me an idea," Joe said. "If I play mugger, will you help me move the tooth to the auditorium? It won't fit in the back of the van. It's practically the size of a car, and it weighs a ton. There's no way to move it that far unless a couple of guys our size get inside it and walk it downtown to the auditorium."

"Sure," Steven said. "It's a deal. We'll walk it over Tuesday afternoon."

"Thanks," Joe said. "And you can count on me for the mugger plan."

"Great," Steven said happily. "And, uh . . . Joe, buddy ol' pal, if you wouldn't mind, come by and mug me, too. I wouldn't mind looking like a hero in front of a certain blond girl who shall remain nameless."

"Trying to get back together with Cathy?" Joe asked with a laugh.

"Uh . . . yeah. Exactly," Steven agreed, trying not to feel guilty for lying to his best friend. "I realized what a mistake I'd made. I figure saving Cathy from a mugging would be a great way to get back together with her. So after you get through mugging Denny and Elizabeth, swing by the corner of Maple and Peach and mug Cathy and me. We'll be ready for action."

Nine

"Why don't I carry my backpack for a while?" Elizabeth asked. It was Saturday, and she and Denny were on their way back from the public library. She had a research paper due next week, and her backpack was full of thick, heavy books about the Roman Empire.

"No," Denny wheezed hoarsely. "I'm fine."

Elizabeth sighed loudly, not even bothering to hide her frustration. He looked exhausted, struggling along under the combined weight of her backpack and his. And he sounded terrible. He'd stood under her window singing for over three hours yesterday—until the neighbors had called the police.

"Sorry I couldn't finish my concert yesterday," he puffed, as if reading her mind. "I didn't know the police would be so strict about enforcing the noise-pollution ban."

"I understand," Elizabeth said.

"I had a lot more material," Denny said shyly. "Some of it rhymed really well. If you want, we could go by my house and I could finish singing all the songs I wrote for you."

"That's OK," Elizabeth said quickly. "I heard plenty. I mean . . . uh . . . I'm touched that you wanted to devote so much time to singing to me, but I, um, don't want to keep you from your homework."

Denny's big gray eyes gazed at her adoringly. "It's the least I could do for somebody who's saved my life. *Twice*."

Elizabeth looked at her watch. Joe would be coming along any minute now. *Please let this work,* she begged silently.

Right at the appointed time, Elizabeth saw the bushes rustle. *Thank goodness,* she thought. She had been a little afraid that Joe might not be a convincing mugger. But as soon as he jumped out of the bushes, she stopped worrying. He looked very menacing in his ski mask and shabby clothes.

Elizabeth let out a little shriek, and Denny gasped in surprise as Joe stood right in front of them, blocking their path.

"Gimme yer jewelry and credit cards," Joe growled.

"Oh no!" Elizabeth cried in a frightened voice.

"We don't have jewelry and credit cards," Denny argued. "We're middle-school students."

"Oh," Joe said blankly. He shifted his weight to his

other foot, clearly at a loss for words. "Then . . . gimme yer lunch money!"

"No!" Elizabeth cried. She shrank against Denny and clutched her purse.

"I said, gimme yer lunch money," Joe growled again. He lurched forward, as if to grab her purse.

Suddenly Denny swung around and pounded Joe in the ribs with her heavy backpack.

"Hey!" Joe cried in surprise and anger.

Denny dropped the backpack and lifted his fists in a boxing stance.

Elizabeth gasped. She'd had no idea that Denny would actually fight Joe.

Denny threw a punch that landed on Joe's shoulder.

"Stop that!" Joe insisted.

But Denny was already winding up his arm again.

"No!" Elizabeth shrieked at Denny.

But it was too late. Denny's fist was already hurtling toward Joe's jaw.

In self-defense, Joe balled up his own fist and socked Denny right in the stomach.

Denny doubled over, but then lurched forward, butting Joe in the stomach with his head.

Joe pushed Denny back and prepared to swing again.

Elizabeth bit her knuckles. This was getting totally out of hand. Joe seemed to have completely forgotten it was just a pretend fight. He was really pummeling Denny.

Denny was definitely getting the worst of it. When

Joe lifted his fist again and aimed it at Denny's nose, Elizabeth sprang into action.

"Stop it!" she screamed, jumping forward and landing on Joe's back.

She reached out, grabbed Joe's hand, and quickly pulled his arm behind his back.

"Ow!" Joe cried.

"Cut it out!" Elizabeth shouted.

"Yeooww!" Joe hollered. "You're going to break my arm." He shook himself violently until Elizabeth's grasp loosened. He gave one final shake, threw Elizabeth off, and then took off running down the street.

Denny slowly picked himself up off the sidewalk. "I can't believe it," he breathed, staring at her in amazement. "It's like some kind of weird destiny thing. You saved me—again."

Denny's eyes began to glow. Elizabeth felt her heart sink right down into her stomach.

"So?" Pam said, tapping her foot.

Steven swallowed hard and wiped the beads of perspiration from his forehead. Where was Joe? He was supposed to be here by now.

"So I pretended to throw the ball, but I really didn't . . . that's called a fake," he explained.

"I know," Pam said impatiently. "I've played basketball before."

"You have? I mean . . . ahhhh . . . of course you have. Ha ha ha." *Stop laughing*, he ordered himself. He hated it when he got nervous and laughed like that. But who wouldn't be nervous under these circumstances? He hadn't counted on having to make small talk for so long. And his basketball stories were obviously not making a big hit.

"Steven," Pam said impatiently. "I have a lot to do. Did you ask me to meet you here today just so you could tell me stories about basketball?"

"Of course not," Steven said quickly. "I asked you to meet you here so . . . so . . . uhhhh." Steven racked his brains for something to say. This wasn't working out at all. The way he'd pictured it, within seconds of Pam's arrival, the mugger would appear. Steven would scare him off with a lot of tough talk, and then Pam would be so grateful and impressed, he wouldn't feel embarrassed to ask her out.

Had Joe somehow figured out that it was Pam and not Cathy that Steven wanted to impress?

Had Joe left him standing here like an idiot on purpose?

Pam stared at him with an expectant look on her face.

"I was just wondering . . . uhhh . . ."

"Wondering what?"

"Wondering if you . . . uhhhh . . . if you and I could . . ."

Suddenly his ears perked up. Far down the street, on the other side of the high hedge, he heard the sound of running footsteps.

It's about time, Steven thought.

Steven stood up straighter. "Hold on a minute, Pam, I think someone is behind that hedge."

"So what?" Pam said.

The footsteps grew louder. Steven placed a protective hand on Pam's arm. "Those footsteps sound like danger to me."

For a moment Pam stared at him as though he were completely deranged, then she shrugged off his hand. "It just sounds like somebody running."

The footsteps were nearing the corner.

"Stand back," Steven said firmly. "I'll protect you."

Pam rolled her eyes. "Protect me from what?"

"Quick," Steven ordered. "Stand here, behind this mailbox, so he won't see you."

"What are you doing?" Pam sputtered as he shoved her behind the big green mailbox. He didn't want Joe to see that it was Pam. Before Steven could answer, Joe came running around the corner of the hedge at top speed.

"Hey!" Steven cried as Joe passed right by him without pausing.

But Joe just kept running.

What's he doing? Steven wondered frantically. They'd gone over the plan three times. Why didn't Joe stop and confront them? What was Steven supposed to do?

Joe was halfway down the block now. Maybe Steven was supposed to chase him. Sure. That was it. Joe was giving him a chance to show off. Steven was the fastest runner on the team.

Wow! What a pal. It almost made Steven feel guilty about tricking Joe into thinking he was trying to get Cathy back.

"Hold it!" Steven shouted in his deepest voice as he broke into a run. "Hold it right there, buddy."

Joe didn't even slow down. Steven's feet pounded against the pavement as he ran. It didn't take him long to catch up. Steven had always been a faster runner than Joe.

Joe turned the corner sharply, and Steven stayed right on his tail. He leaped forward, wrapped his arms around Joe's waist, and tackled him.

"Owwww!" Joe yelled as both he and Steven fell heavily to the ground.

"Get off me, Wakefield!" Joe shouted angrily, shoving Steven off of him.

"What are you doing?" Steven asked, surprised by the antagonism in Joe's voice.

Joe sat up and pushed Steven away. Then he pulled off the ski mask and threw it on the ground. "Getting away from you and your loony sister!" he shouted. With that he jumped up and ran off in the direction of his house.

Steven picked himself up, dusted off his pants, and hurried back around the corner.

Pam had come out from behind the mailbox. She watched his approach with her arms folded across her chest and an impatient expression on her face.

"Steven," she said, "I really have a lot to do, and I don't have time to watch you play around with your friends."

"That wasn't my friend," Steven insisted weakly. "It was a mugger."

Pam's eyebrows flew upward. "Then why were *you* chasing *him*?"

Steven wet his lips nervously. He couldn't think of one single thing to say.

Pam pursed her lips and gave him a disgusted look. "Really, Steven. I would have expected more from the brother of a hero like Elizabeth Wakefield."

Ten

"What do you mean, you got carried away?" Elizabeth, Steven, and Jessica all yelled at once.

They had all agreed to meet back at Joe's house after the mugging. Jessica had been the first to arrive, and she'd been surprised when an angry and bruised Joe Howell had come running up the front walk. Shortly afterward, Elizabeth and Steven had arrived. And both of them were as angry as Joe.

"You said that Denny would just yell and shout," Joe shot back angrily. "You didn't tell me he was going to go right for my stomach."

"We didn't know he would fight back that hard," Steven said defensively.

"Even if he did punch you in the stomach, you didn't have to hit him back," Elizabeth snapped. "You looked like you were going to break his nose."

"I couldn't help it. When somebody goes for my stomach, my instinct is to punch them back." He glared at Elizabeth. "And did you really need to twist my arm so hard you practically tore it off my shoulder?" Joe rolled up his sleeve and pointed to the bruise on his arm. "Look what you did to me."

"I'm sorry," Elizabeth muttered. "I thought you were really going to hurt Denny."

"Whose stupid idea was this, anyway?" Joe asked.

Three pairs of eyes turned accusingly toward Steven.

"Hey, it's not my fault it didn't work," Steven croaked.

"Let's not give up completely," Jessica said quickly, her mind racing. "We'll just have to do it again. And next time, we'll do it like this: Elizabeth will be walking along by herself. Joe will pop out of the bushes and pretend to mug her. She'll scream. We'll be sure Denny is nearby—but not near enough to hit anybody. As soon as Denny runs up, Joe will pretend to get scared and run away." She grinned. "Perfect, huh?"

Three pairs of eyes stared stonily at her.

"All right. So it needs a little work. But at least it's a plan."

Nobody said a word.

"Well, at least I'm trying," Jessica said angrily. "And I don't see anybody else coming up with a plan."

"I don't care what kind of plan you three think up after this," Joe said angrily. "I'm out of the mugger business—for good."

* * *

"We didn't solve the problem. In fact, we're worse off than we were before," Steven said unhappily.

The three Wakefields were sitting on a park bench. They had just left the Howells' house and had decided to stop on the way home to review their situation.

"By the time Denny gets through telling the story and exaggerating the details," Jessica said, "you'll be some kind of legend. The Secret Service will probably offer you a job at the White House."

"You might as well start wearing a cape and changing in phone booths," Steven said.

"Would you guys shut up?" Elizabeth snapped. "This isn't funny."

"You're telling me," Steven said. "I made a complete fool out of myself in front of Pam Martin."

"Janet will never speak to me again," Jessica said glumly.

"Denny is probably home right now, writing some new songs to sing to me," Elizabeth wailed.

"Arrrggggg!" the three of them groaned at once.

Steven put an arm around each sister. "I know things look bleak. But we've got to stay on the same team. Work together. We'll figure something out. We *have* to," he added weakly.

"Come on," Jessica whispered. "This way."

It was early Monday morning, and Jessica and Elizabeth were leaving for school much earlier than usual. The twins had gone downstairs before anyone else, eaten their breakfast without turning on the lights, and then slipped out the back door.

Elizabeth followed Jessica as they tiptoed around the corner of the house with their backpacks over their shoulders.

Very carefully, Jessica peeked around one of the large bushes that flanked each side of the Wakefield home. Then she suddenly backed up.

Elizabeth backed up quickly too. "Is he out there?" she whispered.

Jessica nodded. "He's there all right. Look."

Elizabeth peeked over Jessica's shoulder and groaned. Denny was sitting on the curb across the street from the house. He was obviously waiting for Elizabeth to come out.

This was actually an improvement. Last week, Mr. Wakefield had explained to Denny that they preferred not to have company during breakfast, but he was welcome to wait for Elizabeth outside.

"We're going to have to take the detour again," Jessica whispered. "It's a good thing we got an early start."

Elizabeth nodded and followed Jessica into the backyard. Both girls hurled their jackets, purses, and backpacks over the fence that divided the Wakefields' backyard from the yard behind it. Then they began climbing.

"Darn!" Jessica muttered as she dropped to the ground on the other side. "I just snagged my sweater."

"I'll fix it for you," Elizabeth offered, dropping to her feet beside her sister.

"Don't worry about it," Jessica joked. "You have enough to do, saving Denny three times a day."

"Ha ha," Elizabeth retorted as the two girls made their way through the neighbors' backyard. "But seriously, Jess, I appreciate your coming with me. I just couldn't face walking to school with him one more time. All that gratitude is making me sick."

"Speaking of gratitude, don't be so grateful," Jessica said. "I'm doing this for me as much as you. If Janet saw you walking to school with Denny again, she would probably explode in my face. You know how irrational Janet gets when she's jealous. She's decided this whole thing with you and Denny is my fault."

"So let's just hope Denny keeps the mugger story to himself," Elizabeth said.

"Ohhhhh noooo," Elizabeth and Jessica both groaned at once.

There was a group of boys gathered on the front steps of the school—Denny's friends.

"Denny must have spent all of last night on the phone," Elizabeth moaned. "This is just awful. I feel like a complete phony."

"You're not a *complete* phony," Jessica argued. "Just a two-thirds phony. Don't forget, you saved Denny's life for real two times."

"I'm not sure the second time counts," Elizabeth said. "If I hadn't—"

Before she could finish, the boys spotted her.

"Hey, Elizabeth!" Rick Hunter cried. "I heard about the mugger. Unbelievable!"

"You must have an incredible arm!" Aaron shouted.

"Excuse me," Elizabeth mumbled, trying to move past the group.

"Did he really have a gun?" Scott Joslin asked.

"Of course not, stupid," Charlie Cashman said scornfully. "It was a knife. Right, Elizabeth?"

As soon as Elizabeth stepped in the front door of the school, she was met by Randy Mason and Ken Matthews.

"Hey, Elizabeth!" Randy said. "We were thinking you could give us all a lecture on self-defense."

"Maybe even represent Sweet Valley Middle School at the Teen Health Fair next Sunday, instead of Janet Howell," Ken added in a loud voice. "After all, knowing how to protect yourself is the best way to stay healthy."

There was an outraged gasp, and Elizabeth looked up quickly. Janet stood over by the lockers with several of the Unicorns. They began whispering amongst themselves. Tamara Chase's mouth formed a grim line. Kimberly Haver pointedly turned her back to Elizabeth.

"Yeah!" Randy echoed. "Who wants to hear about orthodontia when you can hear about saving lives?"

"Elizabeth!" she heard a familiar voice shout.

Elizabeth whirled around and saw Denny running

toward her. "I'm sorry," he panted. "I thought I was at your house early enough to pick you up when you left for school. You must have left just before I got there. Here. Let me take your backpack."

"I've got it," Patrick Morris insisted, appearing at her elbow and snatching the backpack from Elizabeth's arm. "Say, this feels pretty heavy. Have you got some kind of weapon in here?"

"No!" Elizabeth cried. Were they crazy? These guys were getting completely carried away.

"Weapon! Are you kidding?" Denny said, pulling the backpack away from Patrick. "All she needs is her bare hands."

Janet's eyes grew even narrower. Elizabeth felt as though they were boring a hole in her back.

Good thing looks can't kill, Elizabeth thought, *or I'd be a goner.* She'd never seen anybody look so angry in her whole life.

It wasn't just the Unicorns that looked mad, either. Some of the girls that Elizabeth liked were looking a little distant too.

Sarah Thomas and Sophia Rizzo stood talking by the water fountain. When Sophia caught Elizabeth's eye, she looked away. Elizabeth sighed. She understood why Sophia was looking so unfriendly. Patrick and Denny were playing tug-of-war with her backpack and arguing over who was going to carry it to class for her. Sophia had a big crush on Patrick. And until today, he had seemed to have a crush on her, too. The two of them had been partners in the middle-school marriage project.

Elizabeth couldn't really blame her. She remembered how awful she had felt when Todd had paid a lot of attention to another girl at the Valentine's Day dance.

Thinking about Todd made Elizabeth's heart sink. Todd was just about the only boy at school who *didn't* want to talk to her. Maybe it was because he was sick of having to fight his way through a crowd of admirers.

Right now he was standing over by his locker, refusing even to look in her direction.

This is so unfair, Elizabeth thought as she snatched her backpack from Patrick and Denny and stalked off toward homeroom.

"I don't know why they're acting like this," Amy said later as she and Elizabeth hurried to their lockers between periods. "All I can tell you is that I've heard the story four times—and each time it was more dramatic." She smiled bleakly. "According to Ken, you single-handedly fought off a bunch of terrorists carrying automatic weapons."

Amy didn't look too happy. Elizabeth knew why. Amy had a big crush on Ken Matthews. It must have been pretty hard for her to listen to Ken go on and on about Elizabeth's bravery when Amy knew the whole mugging thing had been a setup.

"I'm sorry," Elizabeth said. "I really am. But Ken will get over it."

"That's what you said about Denny," Amy pointed out.

Elizabeth shook her head. "If he doesn't stop soon, I'm going to change my name and move to a different town. Then you won't have to listen to people talk about me anymore."

"Good," Amy said with a chuckle. "Because even I'm sick of hearing about you—and I'm your best friend." She shut the door of her locker with a bang, and walked off toward her class.

Elizabeth had just turned back to her locker when Janet Howell appeared beside her. "Boyfriend stealer," Janet hissed.

Elizabeth let out her breath in a long sigh. "I am *not* a boyfriend stealer."

"You are so a boyfriend stealer," Janet snapped. "And you're a show-off. I'm surprised I haven't seen you on the talk shows yet, bragging about what a hero you are."

Elizabeth didn't know whether to laugh or cry. She was the only person who *hadn't* done any bragging about what had happened. "I don't brag," Elizabeth said in a level voice. She struggled hard to sound reasonable. "And believe me, I know I'm not a hero."

Janet's unfriendly face began to relax, and Elizabeth felt a little flicker of hope. She didn't particularly want to be Janet's friend, but she sure didn't want to be her enemy. She knew how much trouble Janet could cause for Jessica. If she could somehow appeal to Janet's sense of reason, maybe Janet would leave them alone.

"My mom says Denny will get over this pretty soon. We just have to be patient. Denny's attachment to me is kind of like an accident," Elizabeth said in a rush. "What I mean is . . . I'm just the person who happened to be with Denny when he was in trouble. If you had been there, you would have done the same things I did. I'm sure of it."

"Not a chance," a voice said from behind them.

Elizabeth and Janet both turned and saw Bruce Patman giving them a smug smile. Bruce was a seventh-grader who thought he was the coolest guy in school.

"I've seen Janet swim. She couldn't rescue a beach ball from the water," he said. "And if she ever saw a mugger—"

"Bruce," Elizabeth said angrily. "We weren't talking to you."

Bruce turned to Janet. "I can't believe that Mr. Clark actually asked *you* to give the lecture at the Teen Health Fair when we have somebody like Elizabeth around."

"What do you mean?" Janet seethed. "Orthodontia is a very important topic."

But Bruce just laughed in her face. "Orthodontia! How lame. Who cares about orthodontia?"

"That does it," Janet fumed as Bruce swaggered away. "I told Jessica that you were making the Unicorns look bad. And this proves it. You're going to be sorry, Elizabeth Wakefield."

Eleven

Jessica hurried across the Howells' front yard toward the garage. Immediately following second period, Janet had announced an emergency after-school meeting of the Unicorns. Jessica had the uncomfortable feeling she knew what the meeting was about.

All the other Unicorns were there when she walked in, and Janet stood in front of the giant papier-mâché tooth that Mary and Mandy had made.

Mandy and Mary were busy touching up the paint on one side of the tooth, getting it ready for Joe and Steven to move the next day.

"Let's get started," Janet said briskly as soon as Jessica closed the garage door behind her. She turned to the group. "As you all know, the Unicorns have a public-relations problem."

"A public-relations problem? I thought we were

here because you were jealous of Elizabeth," Ellen said in confusion.

"Shhhh," Lila hissed.

"Jessica," Janet continued. "It was your job to do something about the problem, and you haven't."

"I tried," Jessica insisted.

"Obviously you didn't try hard enough," Janet said coldly. "Three boys have actually suggested to me that I resign as Sweet Valley's Teen Health Fair representative. They had the nerve to suggest that Elizabeth might be a more interesting speaker than me."

"I can't believe that," Lila said in an outraged voice. She threw Jessica a disgusted look. "And I can't believe you'd let Elizabeth do this to the Unicorns. It's so humiliating."

"There's no serious possibility that I'll be replaced," Janet went on. "Speakers have to be in seventh or eighth grade. But still, it's embarrassing to me and every member of this club to have people even *joking* about it."

"Janet's right," Tamara said.

"And so, Jessica, I'd like you to know you are no longer even *eligible* to be a Teen Health Fair hostess," Janet announced.

"That's not fair!" Jessica protested angrily.

"This is the final decision of the Unicorn Club," Janet responded.

Jessica looked quickly to Mandy and Mary. They were the girls she could usually count on to be reasonable.

Mary shifted uncomfortably when Jessica caught her eye. Then Jessica shot a quick look at Mandy. Mandy shook her head slightly as if to say, *I can't help you.*

"You may, of course, attend the Teen Health Fair on your own," Janet continued. "But you won't have any official standing as a participant. And you're forbidden to wear purple. In fact, you're forbidden to wear purple until further notice . . . unless . . ."

"Unless?" Jessica asked hopefully.

"Unless you find some way to stop this . . . Elizabethmania once and for all."

Jessica gritted her teeth angrily. She was so mad at Janet. So mad at Lila. She was so mad at all of them for ganging up against her. And most of all, she was so mad at Elizabeth.

She couldn't help it. Hadn't Steven and Jessica come up with two foolproof plans for making Denny a hero? And hadn't Elizabeth ruined them both by jumping in to "save" Denny when it probably wasn't even necessary?

As much as she pretended she didn't, Elizabeth probably loved being a hero.

"You should have been there to see it," Pam was saying. "Steven Wakefield is such a weird guy."

Steven was in the library after school, looking through the shelves for some research material. He'd been on the verge of stepping out from behind the shelf when he'd heard his name.

He'd recognized Pam's voice right away. The other

voice he wasn't sure about. But it sounded like the dark-haired girl who sat behind him in English.

"Really? He seems so normal," he heard the dark-haired girl exclaim. "What did he do?"

"On Saturday he called me and asked me to meet him at the corner of Peach and Maple. I know he wanted to ask me out," Pam said in a disgusted voice. "But he just couldn't seem to get up his nerve. Instead of asking me out—like a mature guy—he just freaked out and started doing this really bizarre thing to avoid asking me."

"You're kidding! Steven seems like such a cool guy."

"Well, he sure wasn't very cool yesterday. He got so totally carried away that he tried to convince me that this guy running by was a mugger. Then he took off, chasing him down the street." Pam began to laugh. "It was the most ridiculous thing I've ever seen. You would have thought he was four instead of fourteen."

"Maybe it *was* a mugger," the other girl said quickly. "I heard that somebody tried to mug two kids from the middle school over the weekend. One of the kids fought the mugger off. As a matter of fact, I think it was Steven's little sister, the one who saved that boy from drowning."

Pam snorted in disgust. "How can a girl like that have such a completely goofy brother?"

Steven stood on the other side of the library shelf and cringed. His cheeks were red-hot. He had made a complete and total fool out of himself in front of Pam. He'd never have a chance with her. And now she was telling everybody else what an idiot he was.

It was all Elizabeth's fault, he concluded angrily. She should have just left Denny and Joe alone. So they threw a few punches. Big deal. Neither one of them was exactly world-heavyweight material. How much damage could they have done to each other?

All Elizabeth had succeeded in doing was making herself look like an even bigger hero—and making him look like a total loser!

"Elizabeth, I saw Mrs. Patman at the post office today," Mrs. Wakefield said that night at dinner. "She told me again how impressed everyone was with your quick thinking at the beach."

Elizabeth lifted her eyes from her plate and looked across the table at her brother and sister. Both of them were staring down at their plates.

"That's a coincidence," Mr. Wakefield said. "I ran into Mr. Matthews at the copy center, and he said pretty much the same thing."

Jessica and Steven lifted their eyes and stared frostily across the table at Elizabeth.

Elizabeth lowered her eyes to her plate and brought her fork to her lips. Her forkful of mashed potatoes tasted like a big glob of paste. Nothing tasted good to her tonight. Her brother and sister had been giving her dirty looks ever since they sat down, and it was ruining her appetite.

Mr. Wakefield helped himself to the bowl of peas. "Mr. Parker, the man who owns the office-supply store, has Elizabeth's picture posted on his bulletin board—the picture of her and Denny that was in the paper."

"Isn't that nice," Steven said sarcastically.

Mr. Wakefield handed the peas to Mrs. Wakefield. "I'm not sure I like your tone of voice, Steven."

Steven lowered his eyes. "Sorry," he muttered as his cheeks turned a little pink.

Mrs. Wakefield took a sip of her water and then put her glass down on the table. "I've noticed a distinct chill in the air. Is there something wrong?"

Nobody said a word, and Elizabeth stared determinedly at the food on her plate. Chill was an understatement. Jessica and Steven were obviously furious with her. Elizabeth wasn't sure why. But she guessed they were angry for the same reason everybody else was—they were sick of hearing about how great she was.

"OK," Mr. Wakefield said. "I think I know what this is about. Steven, Jessica. I'm ashamed of you."

Jessica let out a little squeak of outrage, and Steven's frown deepened into a scowl.

"A lot of nice things have been said about your sister recently and the message that's coming through loud and clear is that you're both jealous of her."

"Dad," Elizabeth began to protest. Whatever else he had to say on the subject would probably just make things worse.

"Please don't interrupt me, Elizabeth," Mr. Wakefield said. "Petty jealousy like this makes you look childish," he said, turning his attention back to Jessica and Steven. "Grow up. That's an order."

"Thanks a lot, Elizabeth," Steven said bitterly as they walked through the living room and headed up the stairs.

"Yeah, nice going," Jessica said sarcastically. "You're making me look bad at school. And now you're making me look bad at home."

"I'm sorry," Elizabeth said unhappily. "I'm not trying to make anybody look bad. Why are you two giving me such a hard time? What happened to all that stuff about the three of us working together? What happened to all that stuff about us all being on the same team?"

"It's hard to be on the same team when *you* keep winning and *we* keep losing," Steven said.

Elizabeth felt horrible. Soon she wouldn't have a friend left in the whole world.

Except Denny.

Maybe I better start being nicer to him, she thought glumly. *He's all I've got left.*

Steven was trudging up the steps with Jessica trailing behind him when the doorbell rang.

Elizabeth opened the door. "Joe!" she cried out in surprise.

Steven and Jessica turned around. "What are you doing here?" Steven asked. "I thought you were mad at me."

Joe nodded. "I was. But I've decided not to be mad anymore because I need a favor. Can I study over here with you guys tonight?"

"Sure," Steven replied. "But why?"

"Because Janet's in an even more horrible mood over this Denny stuff. When Janet's in a horrible mood, she screams at my mom. And when Janet screams at my mom, my mom screams at my dad. And when my mom screams at my dad, my dad screams at me. Needless to say, things are pretty loud around our house tonight. I can't get anything done."

"I guess you can thank Elizabeth for that," Jessica said.

Jessica, Steven, and Joe all turned to stare at Elizabeth.

That was it. That did it. She couldn't take it for one more second. *"That does it!"* Elizabeth exploded. She slammed the front door shut. "I've had it with you guys! I've had it with Denny and Janet and everybody else, too! You think I like what's been happening to me? *I hate this!* I wish like anything that Janet had been on the beach that day instead of me! I wish she could have saved Denny and that she was Denny's hero!"

There was a long silence when Elizabeth finished shouting. Everybody looked stunned.

Steven drew in his breath. "Of course! Why didn't I see it before?"

"It's brilliant," Jessica gasped.

"But can we do it?" Joe asked.

For once Elizabeth was two steps behind her brother and sister. She had no idea what they were getting at. "Do what?" she asked. "What are you talking about?"

"Don't you see?" Steven said breathlessly. "We've been going about this thing all wrong. We've been trying to make a hero out of Denny."

Elizabeth nodded. "So? What's wrong with that?"

Steven exchanged a knowing smile with Joe and Jessica. "The person we need to make a hero out of is Janet," Jessica said, unable to suppress a giggle.

"Ahhhhhh," Elizabeth breathed. Of course. It was so obvious. "But how?"

"Come on," Jessica said. "Let's go upstairs. I think I've got an idea. And we're going to need some help to pull it off."

All four of them ran up the stairs toward Steven's room.

"Does this mean we're all on the same team again?" Elizabeth asked hopefully.

"You bet!" Steven answered. "But we're going to need a few more players."

Twelve

"We really appreciate your helping us out," Steven said to Sam Jacobson.

"Are you kidding? I'd do anything for Elizabeth. I really owe her a favor after she saved my little brother's life." He grinned. "Though I have to say, this seems like a weird kind of favor." He draped his roller skates over his shoulder. "Sounds like fun, though."

Maria and Amy grinned. "Let's just hope it works."

"It'll work," Steven assured everyone. He winked at Elizabeth and Jessica. "Everybody clear on the plan?"

Elizabeth nodded. "Amy and I make sure Denny is at the intersection of Fifth Street and Pine, at the end of the Plaza Shopping Strip, at exactly four o'clock."

"And Maria and I make sure Janet's at the same intersection at the same time," Jessica said.

Steven gave the thumbs-up sign. "Great. You guys take care of that. We'll take care of the rest." He looked at Joe and Sam. "Ready to roll?"

Joe laughed and lifted his skates. "Pine Street is the steepest street in town. We'll be rolling, all right. Don't you worry."

Maria dropped the coin in the pay phone and dialed. She signaled Jessica to put her head closer to the phone so she could hear the conversation.

"Hello?" Janet's voice sounded flat and uninterested when she picked up the phone.

"Hi, Janet. This is Maria Slater."

There was a long silence at the other end of the line. Maria and Janet weren't particularly friendly. Jessica could tell that Janet was wondering why Maria was calling.

"Listen, I heard that the photographers are going to take some publicity pictures of you and the other Health Fair speakers tomorrow morning," Maria said in her friendliest, most interested voice.

"That's right," Janet answered.

"Well, I just wanted to call and share a little secret with you that I learned in Hollywood. A makeup technique that all the big-name models and actresses use to look better in their photographs."

"Oh?" Janet sounded very interested now. "That's really nice of you."

"After all, you will be representing Sweet Valley Middle School," Maria said with a laugh. "And the way you look will reflect on all of us."

"That's absolutely right," Janet agreed. "I had no idea that you and I thought so much alike. What's the secret?" she asked eagerly.

"Tapestry Powder in shade number three," Maria answered, naming a fairly common brand of makeup. She shot Jessica a worried look. "Do you have any?"

"No," Janet said thoughtfully. "I don't."

Maria and Jessica smiled in relief. That's what they were hoping she'd say.

"Wouldn't some other kind of powder do just as well?" Janet asked.

"Oh no," Maria went on. "You have to have that particular brand. It has uh . . . uh . . ." She looked to Jessica for help.

"Hydrolypzipolytes," Jessica hissed. There was no such thing, but she hoped Janet wouldn't know that.

"It has hydrolypzipolytes in it," Maria said. "That's a very unique chemical compound that makes your face look smoother and softer and warmer and just really . . . better."

"Hmmmmm," Janet mused. "Maybe I'll pick some up tomorrow morning on my way to the auditorium."

"They carry it at the Plaza Pharmacy. I think you'd better go over there today. *Now*, as a matter of fact. I was just in there a little while ago, and I noticed they had only one package of Tapestry Powder in shade number three left."

"Hmmm. Maybe you're right. I'll go right now," Janet said.

Jessica and Maria grinned at each other and clasped hands. The plan might just work.

"There she goes," Amy whispered.

Elizabeth nodded, watching Janet hurry out of the front door of her house. She and Amy were hidden behind a large tree trunk on the other side of the street.

As soon as Janet started down the sidewalk toward the corner, Joe, Sam, and Steven slipped around the corner of the house where they had been hiding and opened the garage door.

"Let's get moving," Elizabeth said.

The two girls jogged around the corner to the Jacobsons' house, which was on the block behind the Howells'.

Elizabeth and Amy hurried up the front walk and rang the bell. Mrs. Jacobson opened the door and smiled at them. "Elizabeth!" she cried. "What a lovely surprise."

"Hi, Mrs. Jacobson," Elizabeth said. "We just came over to see if Denny wanted to go get some ice cream."

Mrs. Jacobson gave them an apologetic smile. "I'm sure he'd love to go with you girls, but he's not here."

"*Not here!*" Amy and Elizabeth cried together.

Elizabeth was stumped. Denny had been so attentive, she had assumed that if he wasn't with her, he had to be at home. This was terrible.

"Where did he go?" Amy asked quickly.

Mrs. Jacobson adjusted an earring. "Let me see," she mused. "I think he said something about going by the card shop to get you a card. On second thought, he might have been going to the bookstore. Or the gift shop."

"Those are all along the Plaza Shopping Strip," Amy said breathlessly. She grabbed Elizabeth's hand. "Come on."

Elizabeth ran after Amy. "'Bye, Mrs. Jacobson!" she shouted over her shoulder. "And thanks!"

"Uh-oh. Look!" Amy and Elizabeth had run all the way to the Plaza Shopping Strip, hoping to beat Janet Howell. But Janet must have been eager to get to the pharmacy, because she was already crossing the intersection of Fifth and Pine.

"Let's check the card shop!" Amy panted. "Come on."

Elizabeth and Amy hurried into the card shop and ran right into Ken Matthews.

"Hi," he said in a friendly voice.

"Have you seen Denny?" Elizabeth demanded.

"Gee, no. Hey, Elizabeth, I've been wanting to ask you. Do you want to—"

Help! Elizabeth glanced at the clock on the wall. It was ten minutes to four. "Ken," she said quickly, interrupting him. "I'd love to talk. But I've got to run."

She turned so fast her sneakers squeaked on the floor. "Let's check the bookstore," she said to Amy.

"So anyway, I thought maybe you could show me how to break a board with my bare hands," Rick Hunter joked. He had been standing in the comic-book section of the bookstore. As soon as Elizabeth and Amy came in, he'd hurried over.

"Are you sure you haven't seen Denny?" Amy pressed.

Rick shook his head. "No. And I've been here for at least half an hour." He grinned. "What's the matter? Are you worried Denny's not safe without his bodyguard?"

"Ha ha," Amy said dryly.

Elizabeth looked down at her watch. It was two minutes to four. Time was slipping by. "Come on," she urged Amy. "We'll try the gift shop."

Elizabeth and Amy ran out the door and screeched to a halt. "There he is!" Amy shrieked.

Elizabeth's jaw fell open. It was amazing! It was miraculous! Denny was walking toward the intersection. *Right on time.*

Obviously he had stopped by the snack shop, because as he walked, he was munching popcorn from a big bag. A Walkman was clamped to his belt and headphones covered his ears. His head bobbed slightly to the music.

He approached the intersection and paused for the red light. Far away, at the bottom of Pine Street,

Elizabeth saw Steven wave and then dart behind a low, thick hedge.

He was letting her know that everybody was on schedule.

So where was Janet?

"I don't believe this," Maria groaned.

"This is awful," Jessica wailed.

The two girls were peeking through the window of the Plaza Pharmacy. Janet had arrived right on time, purchased her powder, and was now standing in line to pay.

Unfortunately, the line was very long. And it was moving very, very slowly.

"It's almost time," Maria moaned.

"We've got to do something," Jessica insisted.

"Leave it to me," Maria said. "I didn't take all those acting classes for nothing."

"Ohhhhh," Maria groaned, clutching her stomach. She was standing at the magazine rack, not far from the cashier. Several people in line looked over in her direction.

"Arrrggg," she groaned again, doubling over.

"Young lady, is something wrong?" a lady in line asked.

Maria shook her head dramatically and then keeled over.

Immediately all the people in the line hurried over and surrounded her.

Jessica saw Janet move to join them, so she grabbed Janet's arm. "Hi, Janet," she said quickly. "Oh, look. There's nobody in front of you." She practically shoved Janet toward the cashier. "Don't keep the cashier waiting," she urged.

Janet pointed toward Maria. "But Maria Slater just—"

Jessica waved her hand breezily. "Oh, don't worry about Maria. She just ate too much ice cream, that's all. It always affects her like that."

Janet's eyebrows rose in surprise.

"Miss," the cashier snapped. "I'm waiting."

"Oh," Janet said, blushing with confusion. "Here." She put the powder on the counter and the cashier rang it up.

"That's four dollars and twenty-three cents," the cashier said.

Jessica tapped her foot and almost screamed with impatience while Janet fished around for exact change, paid the cashier, and then waited while the cashier put the powder in a bag and stapled the receipt to the top.

Outside the window, Jessica could see Denny standing at the far corner, still waiting for the red light to turn green.

As soon as the cashier held out the bag, Jessica snatched it. "I'll carry it for you," she said lightly.

"But—" Janet began.

But Jessica didn't let her finish. She was already hurrying out of the store.

"Honestly, Jessica," Janet panted as she tried to keep up. "If this is your way of trying to get back on my good side, it won't work—"

A piercing whistle rang out from somewhere down the block.

"Gosh," Jessica said breathlessly, recognizing Steven's signal. "Look over there. That's Denny at the intersection, isn't it?"

The two girls were getting closer now. "You're right," Janet said. "That *is* Denny. It sure is nice to see him without Elizabeth hanging all over him." Then she colored angrily. "Looks like I spoke too soon."

Jessica looked up and saw Amy and Elizabeth approaching from the other direction.

"Let's not even speak to them," Jessica suggested, shoving Janet toward the intersection. "Let's just go say hello to—"

Suddenly the light turned green, and Denny stepped into the intersection.

"Look out! We can't stop!" somebody shouted.

There was a skidding, roaring sound. When Jessica and Janet turned their heads, they saw Janet's giant molar costume skidding down the steep incline of Pine Street on two pairs of roller skates.

"Omigod! It's my tooth!" Janet screamed. "And it's out of control!"

The tooth was picking up speed, going faster and faster and heading right for Denny.

Denny continued on his way across the street, completely unaware of the danger. His head continued to bob up and down to the music of his headset. He never even glanced up.

"Do something, Janet!" Jessica screamed.

"Do something, Janet!" Amy yelled.

"Do something, Janet!" Elizabeth hollered.

Come on, Janet. Come on, Janet, Jessica pleaded silently.

But Janet seemed to be frozen, staring in horror at the giant tooth as it came nearer and nearer.

Just then, Maria came running out of the pharmacy and hurled herself against Amy . . . who slammed into Elizabeth . . . who went careening into Jessica . . . who shoved Janet into the street.

Janet *smashed* into Denny.

"Yeow!" Denny shouted in surprise as the force of Janet's body sent him flying, knocking him out of the way just as the giant tooth went speeding by, narrowly missing Denny and moving so fast it was practically a blur.

Denny and Janet lay on the opposite curb, crumpled up and staring at each other in amazement.

The giant tooth never veered off course when it reached the end of the street. It just kept moving straight ahead, speeding straight toward the thick, bushy hedge.

"Geronimooo!" Jessica heard Joe and Sam yell as the tooth crashed into the bushes and toppled over.

But neither Janet nor Denny seemed to notice. They were too busy gazing into each other's eyes.

"Janet," Denny said in a trembling voice. "I can't believe it. You saved my life."

Janet nodded. "I guess I did." Her voice shook with emotion.

Denny helped Janet to her feet. "How can I ever thank you?" he asked.

Janet stared into his eyes. "You could start by walking me home," she answered.

Jessica and Elizabeth watched them walk away, completely wrapped up in each other, the giant tooth and the face powder completely forgotten.

"Yahoooo!" Elizabeth squealed, giving Jessica a high five.

"We did it!" Jessica shouted.

"Denny has a new hero!" Elizabeth cried out.

"Come on, guys. Get off me," Steven grunted.

Just as they had planned, the thick, leafy bushes had cushioned the impact of the crash, but Steven had wound up being pinned to the ground beneath the giant tooth.

Joe managed to wriggle out and stand up. But Sam was still inside the tooth and he was laughing too hard to extricate himself.

"You guys look hilarious." Joe laughed as he dusted off his jeans. "I wish I had a camera."

"Hi, Joe," a familiar voice called out.

From the ground, Steven looked up and saw Joe's face break into a huge grin. "Hi, Cathy! Hi, Pam!"

Steven groaned inwardly. Oh no. He really hoped the girls wouldn't see over the hedge.

"Hi," Steven heard Cathy reply. "Joe, have you

met Pam Martin yet? She's new. I'm taking her on a little tour of the Plaza Shopping Strip."

"Sure I've met Pam," Joe answered in a confident voice. "We're sort of old friends by now."

Just then, Sam let out more hysterical bursts of laughter, which echoed around inside the cavernous tooth.

"What's that noise?" Cathy asked.

Steven's heart sank. This was the worst. Once again he was caught looking like a total idiot. He saw two familiar faces peek over the hedge. One was Cathy's. One was Pam's.

Pam's eyes widened. She stared for a moment, then shook her head.

Cathy was equally surprised. But instead of looking shocked and disapproving, she began to laugh. "Don't tell me," she said, giggling. "This has something to do with the twins, right?"

Suddenly Steven quit feeling embarrassed. In fact, he started laughing too. One of the great things about Cathy was that she was always ready to appreciate the humor of a situation. He knew she'd roar when he told her how they'd just made a hero out of Janet Howell. *What an awesome girl*, Steven couldn't help thinking.

"Maybe I should take Pam on the tour and let Steven tell you the whole story," Joe suggested.

For once, Steven thought, *Joe has the right idea*.

"Great," Cathy and Steven said at once, waving as Joe and Pam walked off together toward the bookstore.

Cathy leaned down and helped Steven wriggle out from underneath the tooth.

He smiled at her. "I'm sorry I acted like such a jerk," he said contritely.

"That's OK," Cathy said, smiling back. "I'll forgive you for everything if you'll just explain to me how this giant tooth got here. And why Sam Jacobson is inside of it."

Sam started laughing again, and Steven laughed too. "Well, it started like this . . ."

Thirteen

"And in conclusion," Janet said from the podium on the stage. "I would just like to say that proper orthodontia during the teen years can prevent serious dental problems later in life." She smiled out at the audience. "Thank you for your attention. If you have any questions, please stop by the Orthodontia booth and see me. Or you can ask one of the Teen Health Fair hostesses for a flyer."

The audience politely applauded.

Denny clapped enthusiastically and let out a shrill whistle. "Wasn't that a wonderful speech?"

He and the twins were standing in the back of the auditorium. Elizabeth and Jessica exchanged amused glances. Their plan had been a huge success. Over the past week, Denny had been as attached to Janet as he had been to Elizabeth the week before. And unlike Elizabeth, Janet was *loving* it.

"I'm going to escort Janet back to the Orthodontia booth," Denny said. "See you guys later."

"I'd better get out to the lobby and circulate," Jessica said happily. "There are a ton of cute guys here. You wouldn't believe how many of them have come up to ask me for a flyer. I think it's because of the giant tooth. It's really attracting a lot of attention outside the auditorium."

"I'm glad Janet picked you to be a hostess," Elizabeth said. She looked around. "Who else did she pick?"

"Mandy and Mary," Jessica answered. "And Lila, Tamara, and Grace."

Elizabeth frowned as she glanced around the room. "That's funny. I saw Mandy and Mary. But I haven't seen the other three. Where are they?"

Jessica grinned. "Who do you think is inside the tooth?"

Both girls threw back their heads and laughed.

"Janet bribed them by promising to treat them to a movie tonight," Jessica explained. "We're all going to see *The Day the Earth Shook*. It's about an earthquake."

"Yeah, I figured," Elizabeth said. "Actually, I've heard it's really good. Totally terrifying."

"Oh, good," Jessica said. "I love scary movies."

"Try not to get too spooked, though," Elizabeth teased. "After all, you know Sweet Valley is located right over a fault line."

"It is?"

"Sure. Sweet Valley is about as likely to have an earthquake as anywhere in the world."

"Oh, come on, Elizabeth," Jessica said. "We're not going to have an earthquake *here*."

Elizabeth shrugged. "You never know."

Could there be an earthquake in Sweet Valley? Find out in Sweet Valley Twins and Friends #75, **JESSICA AND THE EARTHQUAKE.**

SIGN UP FOR THE SWEET VALLEY HIGH® FAN CLUB!

Hey, girls! Get all the gossip on Sweet Valley High's® most popular teenagers when you join our fantastic Fan Club! As a member, you'll get all of this really cool stuff:

- Membership Card with your own personal Fan Club ID number
- A Sweet Valley High® Secret Treasure Box
- Sweet Valley High® Stationery
- Official Fan Club Pencil (for secret note writing!)
- Three Bookmarks
- A "Members Only" Door Hanger
- Two Skeins of J. & P. Coats® Embroidery Floss with flower barrette instruction leaflet
- Two editions of *The Oracle* newsletter
- Plus exclusive Sweet Valley High® product offers, special savings, contests, and much more!

Be the first to find out what Jessica & Elizabeth Wakefield are up to by joining the Sweet Valley High® Fan Club for the one-year membership fee of only $6.25 each for U.S. residents, $8.25 for Canadian residents (U.S. currency). Includes shipping & handling.

Send a check or money order (do not send cash) made payable to "Sweet Valley High® Fan Club" along with this form to:

SWEET VALLEY HIGH® FAN CLUB, BOX 3919-B, SCHAUMBURG, IL 60168-3919

NAME _____
(Please print clearly)

ADDRESS _____

CITY _____ STATE _____ ZIP _____
(Required)

AGE _____ BIRTHDAY _____ / _____ / _____

1 (800) I LUV BKS!

If you'd like to hear more about your
favorite young adult novels and writers . . .
OR
If you'd like to tell us what you thought
of this book or other books
you've recently read . . .

CALL US at 1(800) I LUV BKS
[1(800)458-8257]

You'll hear a new message about books and
other interesting subjects each month.

**The call is free to you, but please get
your parents' permission first.**